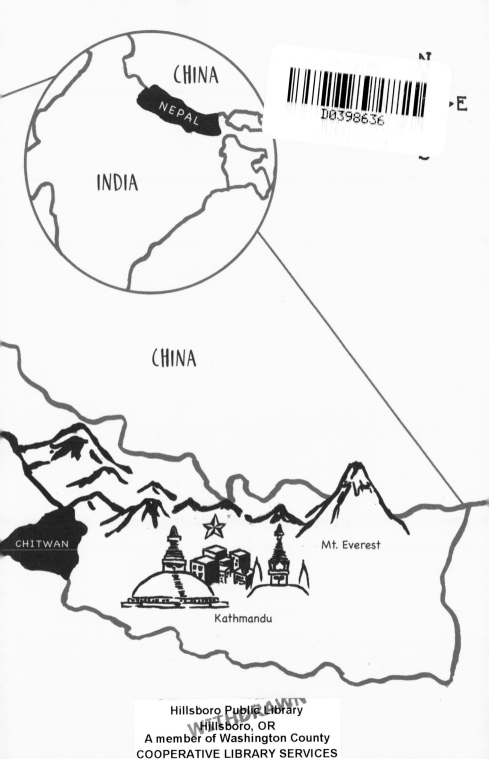

CHINA

NEPAL

INDIA

D0398636

CHINA

CHITWAN

Mt. Everest

Kathmandu

A CIRCLE OF ELEPHANTS

"I loved this book, and read it cover to cover, unable to put it down. It is such a refreshing journey into another elephant world, very special to Asia, indeed Nepal, resonant with an afterglow of Mowgli, and Eric Dinerstein's own deep feelings about the jungle, and the people and the wildlife that live there. It will delight all elephant lovers."

—Iain Douglas-Hamilton, DPhil, CBE, founder,
Save the Elephants, and coauthor of *Among the Elephants*

"Eric Dinerstein has a deep love for and understanding of Asian elephants and the threats and problems they face today. You will be fascinated, angered, and charmed in turn by this beautifully written story. And it will, I am sure, inspire many to help those working tirelessly to protect these wonderful animals and their forest habitat. Please read it and share it with others."

—Jane Goodall, PhD, DBE, founder, the Jane Goodall Institute,
and United Nations Messenger of Peace

"In this fine book, a lifetime of reality-based wisdom is almost magically distilled into the imagined, yearning voice of a young boy in the jungle, surrounded by elephants and tigers and wild things, facing (as we all do) the great question of where he can fit in so changing a world. It's a totally enchanting, utterly unexpected story for children of all ages."

—Carl Safina, author of *Beyond Words: What Animals Think and Feel*

"Eric Dinerstein, a world-class scientist who knows the ecology of the Himalayan region better than almost anyone else, has turned his razor sharp intellect to fiction in his enchanting debut novel, *What Elephants Know*. His deep knowledge of wild animals, lush landscapes, and the rich culture of Nepal permeates through this poignant coming-of-age novel. It's as much fun as bouncing on an elephant back through the swampy tall grass, looking out for the hidden tiger!"

—K. Ullas Karanth, Director for Science-Asia,
Wildlife Conservation Society

A CIRCLE OF ELEPHANTS

ERIC DINERSTEIN

Disney • HYPERION

LOS ANGELES   NEW YORK

First Edition, January 2019

10 9 8 7 6 5 4 3 2 1

FAC-020093-18341

Printed in the United States of America

This book is set in Spectrum MT/Monotype; Qiber/Fontspring
Designed by Maria Elias

Library of Congress Cataloging-in-Publication Data
Names: Dinerstein, Eric, author.
Title: A circle of elephants / by Eric Dinerstein.
Description: First edition. • Los Angeles ; New York : Disney-Hyperion,
2019. • Companion to: What elephants know. • Summary: Thirteen-
year-old Nanda Singh, the youngest elephant driver in Nepal, enjoys a very
special relationship with his tusker, Hira Prashad, through which he grows
in understanding and compassion with all animals, including humans.
Identifiers: LCCN 2018014931 • ISBN 9781368016582 (hardcover)
Subjects: • CYAC: Human-animal relationships—Fiction. •
Elephants—Fiction. • Jungle animals—Fiction. • Jungles—Fiction. •
Orphans—Fiction. • Nepal—History—20th century—Fiction.
Classification: LCC PZ7.1.D57 Cir 2019 • DDC [Fic]—dc23
LC record available at https://lccn.loc.gov/2018014931

336140808769989

Reinforced binding

Visit www.DisneyBooks.com

To those who defend the lives of rhinos,
tigers, and elephants

Be kind to all living creatures.
This is the true religion.
—Buddha

Until one has loved an animal,
a part of one's soul remains unawakened.
—Anatole France

PROLOGUE

I once heard a story about a lonely elephant.

The elephant lived in a mountain forest bordering a great ocean. Many elephants had lived in this forest, but now there was only one—an old male with giant tusks. The others had been killed for their ivory. Poachers tried several times to trap the old male, too, but they could not. The hunters soon feared the tusker, believing that he was a spirit elephant, too dangerous to approach.

A game warden learned of the spirit elephant and began to track him. The warden was determined to protect the animal. He watched as the tusker spent his days wandering the forest, calling out to the others and listening for their trumpets in return. But none called back.

One day the elephant climbed to the top of a ridge. He trumpeted to his lost family. Again, no one answered. Then the elephant entered a clearing with a view of the sea. The warden stayed nearby, unafraid, as the elephant looked out to the ocean. The air vibrated around him, but the warden could not make out any sound. He followed the elephant's gaze with his binoculars. Why would this powerful elephant stare out to sea, rumbling deeply to no one?

Far away, the warden spotted a pod of humpback whales migrating along the coast. They broke the surface and rose high into the air before splashing back into the water. Had the whales called back to the elephant?

The tusker stayed on the ridge for a week. The pod remained along the coast as well. Maybe, the warden thought, the whales stayed so long to comfort the lonely male.

I think of this elephant often. I have even told his story to Hira Prashad, my giant tusker who leads our stable. There is a feeling in me, one so deep I cannot name it. I believe Hira Prashad feels it, too. That our purpose in life is to look out for each other. We are brothers. And together, Hira Prashad and I must watch over the other animals that live at the mercy of humans.

We must answer the call of the lonely trumpeters.

—Nandu, the king's elephant driver,
  Thakurdwara, Nepal

PART 1

DROUGHT

ONE

To ride on elephant back is to float above the world. It is to be with the birds and the monkeys in the trees, where their whistles and hoots ring in your ears. Gliding above the dirt and dust is a privilege—especially for me, a thirteen-year-old Tibetan orphan, and the youngest elephant driver in all of Nepal. It is only when I get down from my elephant that the trouble starts.

On New Year's Day, I rode with my tusker, Hira Prashad, to the highest point along the Great Sand Bar River, two hours north and west of our elephant stable. This spot is called Lalmati, named for its red clay cliffs. The view along the riverbank is like a painting: Bright green cattails sway in the foreground; behind them, white sandbars reach out to the ocher bluffs and rippling water.

We paused at the top of the cliffs to take in the moment.

To me, this is the most beautiful place in the Borderlands jungle—as wild and far from people as you can find. Maybe the isolation is the source of the real beauty. I think this place is Hira Prashad's favorite, too. He rumbles each time we approach it.

"This will be our tradition," I said as I rubbed the top of his head. "On New Year's Day, we will come to these cliffs."

Hira Prashad flapped his ears and lifted his trunk to the river.

It had been almost six months since Dilly, my closest friend, and I found Hira Prashad. He was being starved to death, chained to a tree in the courtyard of the local landlord we call the Python. The sight of the elephant's thin body and sunken eyes was too much for us to bear. Dilly and I bargained with the Python to sell us Hira Prashad. We saved my tusker's life that day—and he has never forgotten it.

The Nepali New Year is a day to celebrate and thank the gods. It is now also the day we mark our brotherhood.

On my command, Hira Prashad dropped to his knees and rolled to his side so I could climb off his back. He rose to his feet again and began grazing in the grassland, ripping the tall shoots with his curled trunk and stuffing them into his mouth. My tusker was hungry. He ate and ate while I wandered. Soon I heard the dull thuds of elephant dung hitting the ground behind me. Fortunately, the smell was sweet, like the grass elephants eat.

I made my way to the edge of the cliff. The swift current of the river swept along far below me. There had been no rain for months, but even in this drought, the depth here was over my head. The cold clear water of the Great Sand Bar River is fed by the melting snows of the high Himalayas, straight north from where I stood.

In the middle of the river, near a maze of sandbars, two narrow, half-submerged logs began to roll. I focused my binoculars to discover they were female *gharial*, the rare ancient crocodilian that still lives along this river. Like a dinosaur, the *gharial* has scaly peaks along its back and a long thin snout to grab fish out of the river.

I scanned the far bank, beyond the *gharial*, where movement caught my eye. The rising heat waves made it difficult to see clearly, but I knew it was a wild elephant, a female, with a small calf. Both were looking up at us on the ridge.

I have heard stories that when an old elephant dies at our stable, she is reborn in her next life as a wild elephant that lives across the Great Sand Bar River. I wondered if that young calf was my elephant mother, Devi Kali—the only mother I have ever known, who died over a year ago. I hoped it was her, enjoying her next life.

Suddenly I felt Hira Prashad at my side. I never cease to be amazed at how quietly elephants can move. The pads under their feet absorb all sound. "Look, Hira Prashad," I said. "That may be our mother across the river." Devi Kali, I had learned, was Hira Prashad's mother, too. He had been separated from her as a baby, just as I had been separated from my birth parents.

Hira Prashad's soft rumbling turned into a long grumble, ending with a loud trumpet.

"What is it?" The roar from the river made it difficult to hear, but I thought the wild elephant had trumpeted as well. Hira Prashad rumbled again and stepped forward, wrapping his trunk around my chest and pulling me backward. I cried out. But Hira Prashad ignored me. He had never done such a thing before.

"*Chii! Chii!*" I shouted the elephant command to let me go and kicked my legs as hard as I could. I was helpless and terrified that Hira Prashad was going to toss me into the river. He grabbed me even tighter around the waist with his trunk. "What are you doing, Hira Prashad?" I yelled. For the first time ever, I was afraid of my brother elephant.

I struggled to free myself, slapping at his trunk. He carried me twenty feet from the cliff's edge before he put me down and started swinging his trunk, herding me back from the cliff. Hira Prashad's angry rumbles kept me moving back farther and farther. Our roles had reversed. The elephant was commanding the driver. Scared, I took giant steps backward. I could not believe he would hurt me, but in my mind I heard the words of my father, *Subba-sahib*, the officer in charge of our stable. "Remember, Nandu, our elephants are still wild animals; we must humble ourselves to ride them."

Hira Prashad pushed me into the grassland. I was so confused, I failed to notice the dead silence—no peacocks, wild jungle fowl, or hornbills calling. Only seconds ago they had all been wailing. A nearby herd of spotted deer, over a hundred of them, stopped barking and stood at attention. At first, I thought they were watching the lone wild dog, the *dhole*, that I saw darting through the clearing. But the deer seemed focused on something else. Hira Prashad sensed it, too. He banged his trunk on the ground and let out a screech I had never heard from an elephant.

"Hira Prashad?!" I yelled. "What do you know that you are not telling me?"

Just as I spoke, every tree around us started to shake. My head nodded up and down, and my arms wiggled left and right. I moved toward my elephant but lost my balance as the earth swayed beneath my feet. I stumbled and fell. Hira Prashad lifted me up and pulled me farther into the grassland. I heard a loud ripping as the place where I had been standing, the entire cliff's edge, collapsed into the river. Two trees bent over and fell, tearing the ground with their huge roots as they landed. The entire jungle trembled. More of the cliff sheared off and crashed into the river.

Hira Prashad curled his trunk around me and held me to his leg, just as Devi Kali did when I was small. I pressed my face into his rough warm skin, praying to the Goddess of the Forest, the one we call Ban Devi. I pleaded with her to make it end. Instead, another great silk cotton tree went crashing down over the edge. The jungle was caving in around us and no one could stop it.

TWO

The last rocks fell from the cliffs. Finally, the earth stopped moving. The air was still and drained of energy. All the animals remained spooked. In the center of the grassland, the herd of spotted deer darted right, then left, unsure of which way to go. Not Hira Prashad, though. He knelt, calm and confident, encouraging me to climb onto his back to return to camp.

Riding atop my elephant, I leaned forward to hug him. "Hira Prashad, now we have saved each other." I held him tightly, my head pressed against his head. "We lost our mother, but found each other." Tears ran down my face and onto Hira Prashad. He reached his trunk over his head to stroke my hair. Moments ago, I thought he had gone mad. Now his gentle touch made my tears run faster than the Great Sand Bar River.

I did not need to guide Hira Prashad home. He knew the trail by heart, either by smell or memory I do not know. *Subba-sahib* once said to me, "Nandu, elephants are never lost in the jungle. They remember every tree they pass, unlike people. We lose our way as easily as chickens."

I covered my face with a headscarf and sprawled out on my tusker's back. I was exhausted. The gentle rhythm of my elephant's pace quieted my fears and lulled me to sleep. When I woke, we were within a mile of the stable.

As we approached camp, Hira Prashad rumbled to the other elephants. They rumbled back excitedly, their trunks swaying and snorting. I imagined they were sharing stories of what had happened.

The drivers were doing the same. Everyone had gathered around the campfire pit to tell their version of the earthquake. A few drivers were shaking their bodies, laughing at each other reenacting the scene. Like me, they had never experienced something that felt like the end of the world.

"Nandu, are you all right?" It was Rita, Dilly's younger sister. She was standing next to her mother, Tulsi. Dilly was crouching by the fire pit, talking to the other drivers.

"Yes, but I had a close call," I said as I climbed down from Hira Prashad to walk him over to the tethering area. Rita followed me. "Are you okay?"

"I am fine," Rita said. "You were the only one out in the jungle. All the other elephants had returned from grazing and—"

"Were you worried about me, Rita?" I loved to tease her. When we were younger, we were rivals. She would beat me climbing trees and I would beat her in our footraces. But ever since she came up with the idea for an elephant breeding center—an idea that saved our stable from closing—I have had a great respect for her. But I did not show it.

"Nandu," she said, grabbing my arm. "What do you mean 'a close call'?"

"Hira Prashad saved me from falling off the cliff. He lifted me out of danger with his trunk!"

"You were so lucky, Nandu. We could have lost you, and I would have no one to race against." She hugged me tight, which I did not expect. Neither did Hira Prashad, who called out to her from his post. "You are brave, too, Hira Prashad!"

At the fire pit, my father had joined the group. I was anxious to tell him that a wild elephant and her baby, who may have been Devi Kali, had warned Hira Prashad to save me. At least, that was how the event now appeared to me.

"Nandu, I am glad you are safe and I am happy to see you. We heard on the radio that the earthquake was very bad in Kathmandu," my father announced. "Had it been much stronger, the capital would be rubble. No reports yet from other parts of Nepal. Let us hope they were equally lucky."

We Nepalis believe in omens—both good and bad. An earthquake on the first day of the New Year was a bad omen. Very bad. Our people stay in their houses all day if a black cat crosses their path. After the earthquake, I wondered if some people might stay inside for a month.

My father gathered the seventy-five men who look after our twenty-five elephants. Each elephant had three drivers to look after it. "Drivers, we have had earthquakes before in the Borderlands. I have lived through three of them myself, all praise to Ban Devi." He tried to lift our spirits. "Let us offer thanks to the Goddess of the Forest that once again she protected us and our stable."

The men murmured in approval. My father was not only *Subba-sahib*, the leader of the stable, he was also a shaman, a spirit doctor, so we did little without seeking Ban Devi's blessing. *Subba-sahib* did not linger on the earthquake. "We have much work to do for the arrival of our new elephants. The day they come will mark the moment we truly become a royal breeding center and nursery for the king's elephants. Let us show our gratitude by attending to our future."

Everyone nodded and grew calmer. I could see why my father is *Subba-sahib*. He never panics.

"Nandu, I cannot wait to drive the new elephants," Dilly whispered to me. We were standing at the back of the group with Rita.

"You cannot ride them, Dilly," Rita said. "They need to be free from work to nurse their newborns."

Dilly pretended to look annoyed at his sister, who was three years younger than him. Rita was fond of telling us what was right and wrong. I did not mind half as much as Dilly did. Rita *was* rather an expert about mothering wildlife. She already cared for the two orphaned rhino calves in our camp as if she were a trained biologist. Father Autry, my teacher and a great biologist himself, had said so. I was sure *Subba-sahib* would assign Rita to help the drivers look after the youngest elephant calves, too. Dilly would have to get used to her authority.

"Now," my father continued, "we shall make the New Year's celebration stretch for several more days while we prepare for the calves and their mothers."

The drivers cheered and whistled. Rita joined in with a whoop. We Nepalis may be superstitious, but we are also brilliant at making a holiday out of any turn of events. People from other countries could take a lesson from us on this point.

His talk finished, my father found me and grasped my shoulder with his one hand. He lost his other arm to a tiger many years ago. He looked into my eyes. "You are not hurt, Nandu?"

"No," I said. "Hira Prashad took me to safety."

He nodded as if this was to be expected. My father has great faith in animals, especially elephants. I wanted to tell him right away about the wild elephant, but then I thought, better to wait until after dinner, when we were alone. He could explain to me what happened like no one else.

We sat in a circle around the campfire with the older drivers sipping tea. Some of the chairs around the fire had been salvaged from a school. They had wooden arms that were perfect for resting one's head, if you were tired enough, which is what I did while I waited for the talking to end.

After all of the drivers had drifted off to bed, my father and I were finally alone.

"*Subba-sahib,*" I began. "Something incredible happened today."

"Something more incredible than an earthquake, Nandu?"

"Yes. I think so. I was standing on the edge of Lalmati, watching two *gharial* through my binoculars, when Hira Prashad came up behind me, wrapped his truck around me, and pulled me away from the edge. Within a minute, the earthquake began, and the place where we were standing broke off and slid a hundred feet down. I would have died."

My father held my gaze with his dark brown eyes. They sparkled like gold in the light of the fire. Then he spoke. "You must take me to the spot tomorrow. We will offer our thanks to Ban Devi."

"And we must thank Devi Kali, too," I murmured.

"Why is that, Nandu?"

"Nothing. I will tell you tomorrow."

My father is not the type to hug, but as I stood, he stood, too, and wrapped his one good arm around me and held me to his chest. I am a copper-skinned boy from Tibet, the land of snow north of the great Himalayas. My father is a dark-skinned Tharu from the vast steamy jungles of the plains at the mountains' base. Our tribes rarely meet, let alone become family, but fate brought us together the day my father found me alone in the jungle, guarded by *dhole*. Now we are father and son, blood tie or no blood tie. Just the way Devi Kali, the elephant who raised me in the stable, was my mother. She is no longer here to hug me with her trunk, but my father is, and his one-armed hug, to me, is the best feeling in the world.

THREE

My father and I left the stable at dawn without saying a word to the other drivers. He wore his canvas bag around his waist, the one he takes to his place of shaman worship in the jungle, where he prays to Ban Devi for the well-being of our elephants and their drivers.

Subba-sahib believes that all living things have souls separate from their bodies, souls that are at one with the great force of nature that is Ban Devi. To him it is always urgent to pray to Ban Devi. In our religion, we believe that nature, animals, humans, and the earth itself all try to live in balance. Part of keeping that harmony is to acknowledge the power of the spiritual world—especially after surviving danger or illness.

Hira Prashad stopped to drink in what was left of the Belgadi River that flows past our camp. My father and I waited while he lowered his trunk and sucked in gallons of water before tipping back his head and releasing the gusher into his mouth. Five times he repeated this to quench his deep thirst.

"Have you ever seen the Belgadi this low, *Subba-sahib*?" I asked.

"Not in thirty years," my father replied quietly.

The drought was not as apparent in the flow of the Great Sand Bar River, where I had spotted the *gharial* yesterday, because its source is the snow of the Himalayas. But the Belgadi is a tributary, and relies on rain to replenish it. It was mid-April, not even the height of the hot and dry season, yet the Belgadi was already reduced to a foot of water trickling down to India. In the summer monsoon, the river is so high that our elephants can barely swim across it.

"What is it, *Subba-sahib*?" Away from the other drivers, when we were all alone, I sometimes called him father. But the deep look in his eyes told me I should call him Shaman.

"Nandu, I had a vision last week. I saw that this drought will not end soon. There will be no monsoon this year."

As if to join in our conversation, a hawk cuckoo started its shriek, which grows louder and louder with every cry. In the hot weather, it sings all day. The British who occupied India called it the brain-fever bird. The men could not stand the heat, and the constant racket from the hawk cuckoo drove some officers mad.

"Maybe the male sings extra loud and long during a drought," I said.

21

"There may be truth to that, Nandu," my father replied. "The farmers must see rain in a few weeks or there will be a poor rice harvest. The animals will start to suffer, too, without water. And the fruit on the trees will dry up."

The signs of drought were everywhere in the jungle. Green leaves, only recently flushed, drooped to keep the sun off their surface. They seemed to whisper as we went by, *we are so thirsty, we are so thirsty*. Even the flowers fell off the crape myrtle trees like a white rain of dry, delicate petals.

When we reached the Lalmati cliffs, Hira Prashad stopped well back from the jagged edge. The red soil and rock made the sheared edge look like a deep wound in the earth. I guess, in a way, it was.

My father coughed. I could see he was taking deep breaths to keep his emotions from overtaking him. This almost never happens. I did not know if he was feeling awe at the power of nature and Ban Devi, or if he was imagining what would have happened to me if Hira Prashad had not been there.

Hira Prashad let out several deep rumbles. I looked at my father, who nodded, as if Hira Prashad had spoken to him. I do not have the skills of my father. And I am sure that Hira Prashad understands me much more than I understand him.

"Did Hira Prashad tell you about the wild elephant across the river?" I asked.

My father looked at me and shook his head.

"*Subba-sahib*, there was a female with a calf across the river. Over there." I pointed to the spot where they stood, just behind the blur of the heat rising off the sandbars. "This was not an illusion, I swear to you. The female lifted her trunk. She trumpeted and moved her head. Like she was warning us."

"Nandu," *Subba-sahib* said. "I think the elephants were confirming what they each felt. Elephants can sense beyond the reach of our own abilities, you know. Not just where to cross a flooding river or how to avoid a patch of quicksand. Elephants notice events before they happen. That is how Hira Prashad saved you. He knew what was to come."

"They were talking about the earthquake?"

"Yes, I believe so."

"That calf she had with her," I said. "I remembered the story about elephants from our stable being reborn in the wild across the Great Sand Bar River. *Subba-sahib*, I think that young calf was Devi Kali trying to protect us, her sons."

I had never spoken to my father of Devi Kali as my mother and Hira Prashad as my brother. But he nodded, knowing this to be the truth. "No doubt you are right, Nandu. I do not think the spirit of Devi Kali would travel outside the Borderlands, especially as long as you are here."

It had not occurred to me before, but I wondered then why Devi Kali would choose to be born wild. For the first time, I questioned if she had enjoyed her life in our stable. My heart grew heavy. I had always believed my fate at the stable was the same as the elephants' fate. That we had been lucky. Maybe the luck was mine, but for the elephants, their fate was different.

My father and I climbed down from Hira Prashad and let him graze. It was time for my father to perform his ritual of gratitude. He chanted and bowed and brought his palms together in the *namaste* gesture. He lit incense and sang words I did not recognize. I usually find Father's rituals strange. In fact, I usually look forward to them being over, but this time I closed my eyes and added my own thoughts and gratitude to Ban Devi for giving me a spiritual elephant family and a shaman for a father.

When my father was finished, Hira Prashad walked over to us, knowing it was time to leave. I hugged my elephant's trunk and began to tremble. I whispered in his ear, "Hira Prashad, I will always protect you like you protected me." Hira Prashad bobbed his head and grumbled. He understood. My father and I climbed onto his back and headed to the stable.

"Let us return by the riverbed," my father said. "In this heat, Hira Prashad will need to drink even more before we head through the jungle."

I steered Hira Prashad gently with my toes behind his jowls, and he moved effortlessly down the trail from the cliff edge leading to the river. We headed south along the Great Sand Bar River for five miles. Hira Prashad stopped to drink twice. Near the edge of the riverbank, we came upon a man with a long black beard and his son huddled around a small fire. They wore plaid *lungis*, the wraparound sarongs of Indian fishermen. The boy crouched with his back toward us, coaxing the coals into flame. Above the fire was a drying rack skewered with small fish. I waved to the older man. He stared back at us like he had never seen a tusker.

I am used to people looking at Hira Prashad. My father says our bull has the longest tusks of any male elephant in Nepal. The boy stood up and stared, too. He had dark features and a narrow face; he looked about my age but was very thin, with bird bones. I have the broad body of a Tibetan and the thick muscles of an elephant driver.

I greeted them in Hindi—*Ram Ram!*—and asked how the fishing was. They said nothing and fixed their gaze on us and my elephant's tusks. It was unusual for them to ignore our greetings. That is when I noticed their shoes: blue canvas sneakers with white laces. Not many in our village wore shoes.

Once Hira Prashad finished drinking, we turned from the bank and headed toward the vast grassland between the Great Sand Bar River and the Belgadi.

"*Subba-sahib*, who were they?"

"I have not seen them before, Nandu."

"Did you notice their shoes?"

"Yes, I do not think they are fishermen. Our fishermen would never ruin shoes going in and out of the water all day." My father chuckled, as he often finds people foolish. He prefers elephants. Like me.

Because my father did not seem concerned, I dropped the subject of their shoes. This fact bothered me, but perhaps I was jealous because I had none.

Up ahead we saw a familiar friend standing proud in the middle of the grassland. The massive black horn of our jungle's enormous male rhino gleamed in the sun. His horn was nearly one and a half feet long. A pair of jungle mynahs were perched on his back.

"Good morning, Pradhan!" I said.

Pradhan swiveled his ears, first one, then the other, at the sound of my voice. Or maybe he heard Hira Prashad's rumble. *Pradhan* means *mayor* in our language, and this male rhino, the largest in the Borderlands, had been here since I learned to ride an elephant.

Pradhan was the first rhino I could name by sight. I was very attached to him, but under no illusion that he felt the same way about me. When I was a young stable hand, not even a *mahout*, I went out to cut grass for the elephants. The drivers dropped me off and left to graze the elephants nearby. No one saw Pradhan in the tall grass.

I was alone when the old male rhino came out of the grass and snorted at me. The drivers sitting on the backs of their elephants stood up and shouted, "Run, Nandu, run!" But it was too late. I could never outrun a rhino. I covered my head and prepared to be trampled and gored.

Pradhan lowered his head and grabbed a wild cane with his upper lip. He had no interest in crushing a naïve stable boy. I was no rival to him. The mayor did not need to prove his strength to me. We both knew that. Ever since that day, Pradhan was family to me, too.

"How old is Pradhan, *Subba-sahib*?"

"He is as old as I am, I suppose. Maybe a bit younger, with a few less wrinkles," he said, laughing. My father was at least fifty years old, but like most Tharu, he does not know his age exactly. Age is not a detail that matters to the Tharu.

Pradhan's skin looked like armor specially crafted for rhinos. He gave us a good, long look, then went back to ripping up the grass blades with his curved upper lip. Pradhan knew us well from grazing our elephants here during the day while we cut grass, and he was used to Hira Prashad. As long as we did not make any sudden moves, we could approach within a few feet of him.

"*Subba-sahib*, the king of all elephants in Nepal and the king of all rhinos are very trusting."

"Yes, they are calm. They pose no danger to each other."

A bigger threat to Pradhan were the other male rhinos who often challenged him to take over the top spot. Pradhan was blind in one eye and walked with a slight limp, but he held his own in battles. Just to let us know he was still king, Pradhan snorted loudly.

I turned and looked at my father. "*Subba-sahib*, do you think that Hira Prashad has the largest tusks of any elephant in Nepal? Wild or living in a stable?"

"I do. Ramji says he has heard of a wild male with even bigger tusks that roams the Kailali jungle on the other side of the Great Sand Bar River. But we know Ramji drinks too much and tells tales."

"Maybe there is an elephant with bigger tusks in Nepal, but none braver than our Hira Prashad!" I said, loud enough for my tusker to hear. He thumped his trunk on the ground, a thing he does when he is excited.

The sun was higher in the sky and the air was unbearably hot. If only it would rain. All the birds had stopped singing, except for the brain-fever bird still shrieking its song from the treetops. A half hour later, thirsty and tired, we were happy to see the smoke from burning elephant dung rising above our elephant stable. The tall evergreen mango trees that encircled camp made it look like an oasis. I was glad to be back home and let out a loud sigh of happiness that got lost in Hira Prashad's trumpeting of our return to camp, which he always did, as if we were royalty.

FOUR

The shock of the earthquake—and fear of bad luck—had tumbled away within a week and our daily routine was back in place. Indra, the *mahout* for Hira Prashad, and I left the stable in the heat of the afternoon to search for grass for our elephants' evening meal. The drought had dried the grasslands and it was becoming harder to find the tender shoots our elephants liked.

Our drivers had set fires to create new growth. They do this to copy nature, which uses fire the same way to hurry things along. Among the charred stems, there were already bright green shoots poking up like a thin carpet. If only we would get a little rain, the carpet would thicken. But there was not a raincloud in sight. The drought had the jungle by the throat like a tiger on a deer.

Up ahead I saw a figure bending over near the edge of the forest. I squinted to see if it was one of our stable boys. The high-pitched bleating of a young animal suddenly pierced my ears. It was the sound an animal makes when caught by a leopard.

"*Agat! Agat!*" I shouted, urging on my tusker. But he did not need a command. Hira Prashad moved so fast we were at the edge of the forest in less than a minute. It was the fisherman's boy from the river! On the ground in front of him were a dozen wire snares, and struggling in one of them was a spotted deer fawn, no more than two months old. It tried to stand and fell to the ground.

"What are you doing here?" I shouted at him.

"Babu, please," he pleaded in Hindi, bowing on his knees before me and holding his hands clasped in front of him. "My family is starving. I have six younger brothers and sisters. My father has run away and left us."

Indra jumped off our tusker to free the spotted deer fawn. I climbed down to help him. The fawn jerked about so much I was afraid she would pull her leg out of joint. Indra held her down while I freed her from the snare. The fawn would not survive the night among the jackals and leopards with an injured leg. I stroked her fur, and she started to calm. The fawn knew Indra and I, at least, meant no harm.

While our backs were turned, the boy took off running.

"Indra, I am going after him!" I shouted, and headed into the forest. I ran fast and caught sight of him. He had crashed into a dense thicket of spiny acacia vines and was caught.

"You! How could you hurt a fawn?" I shouted.

I picked up a stick and whacked at the thicket. The boy whimpered in fear and shut his eyes. I was panting and furious. I slapped the stick hard at his feet. The stick snapped from the force of my blow.

Behind me Hira Prashad rumbled in anger.

I grabbed the boy by the shirt and whipped out my grass-cutting blade. The boy cringed, expecting the worst, but I used my blade to free him from the thorny vine. He was scratched and bleeding all over from the sharp thorns, but too scared to run again with my elephant so close.

"Go back to where you came from. Never come here again!" I shouted.

The boy slipped away into the forest.

I went back to where Indra was standing, cradling the fawn in his arms. My tusker followed behind me.

"Look, Nandu." Indra pointed to two snares on the ground. While he held the fawn, I searched for more. Along the forest edge, where the spotted deer liked to graze, I found fifteen wire snares. Fortunately, they were empty.

"Nandu, you let him go?"

"He is gone for good," I said.

"How do you know that?" Indra asked.

"Because I do."

We reached the edge of the stable with me walking next to Hira Prashad. He had dropped his bundles of grass in the excitement when he came crashing through the forest to find me. We would have to go back and reload. But first we had to find a new home for the fawn.

Indra was holding her close to his chest. He was already attached to the fawn, I could see. There is no animal in the jungle cuter than a baby spotted deer. I waved to Rita, who was standing by the cookhouse when we returned. She ran over, followed by Ritu and Rona, the two orphaned rhino calves she was raising as part of our family at the stable.

"We found her caught in a snare," I said. Rita took the fawn from Indra's arms and carried it toward the cookhouse. Tonight the two rhinos would share their milk bottles with the fawn.

I saw my father hobbling back to his bungalow. His gout was bothering him again.

"Nandu, if this gout keeps troubling me, you will have to take over as *Subba-sahib* sooner than I had planned." I wanted to share in his joke, or even show how flattered I was by him thinking of me in this way, but I could not at this moment.

"*Subba-sahib*, I have something important to tell you."

"You did not feel another earthquake, I hope." His eyes twinkled. He loved to tease me and normally I loved it, too.

"Look at the new member of our stable," I said. Rita had brought the fawn out of the cookhouse and the tiny spotted deer was sniffing the two rhinos who were sniffing her.

"Where did you find this fawn?"

"*Subba-sahib*, remember the boy and the bearded man along the river? The ones wearing the shoes? We caught the boy setting snares. He had just caught the fawn and had set fifteen more traps."

"Where is this boy now?" my father asked. He spoke to me in a sharp tone and instantly I realized that I had made a mistake. Two mistakes really. I never should have threatened to hit him with the stick. Instead, I should have brought him here. My father or the warden could have questioned him. I decided not to tell my father about threatening the boy. What I had done was bad enough.

"He ran away. I should not have let him go."

"It has been many years since anyone has come into the jungle to kill. Let me see our new fawn, Nandu. I know you meant well and you saved her life. We must be more vigilant now."

My stomach churned at the thought of more poachers.

I went back to the cookhouse to help Rita. "Come, Nandu. You hold her while I give her the bottle," Rita said. She was a magical mother to animals. Her dark eyes focused on the fawn's face. She rubbed it between its ears while coaxing the bottle into its mouth, humming a soft song. After a few tries, the exhausted fawn started to drink.

That afternoon I went to resume my studies with my tutor, Father Autry. He had been my teacher at the boarding school in the city my father had made me attend for two semesters. Now Father Autry had retired to the Borderlands. We were both happier here.

Hira Prashad and I approached my tutor's bungalow. A tall, skinny Tharu man walked quickly up the path ahead of us. He carried a small knapsack on his back, which was all he wore aside from a bright white loincloth. He also carried a long, pointed spear in his hand that bobbed up and down as he walked. To my surprise, he went straight through Father Autry's gate.

I left Hira Prashad to snack on banana leaves and entered the gate. Through the open door, I saw Father Autry sitting across his breakfast table from the man, who was so wrinkled and slender he looked like he was a hundred years old. The man's spear was resting against the wall next to a wooden crucifix, a symbol of Father Autry's religion. In the shadow of the cross cast by the sun through the window, a gecko clung to the wall, its orange toes spread wide.

"Nandu, welcome," Father Autry said, having spied me there. "I was just asking my friend about the origin of his spear. He said in the old days he used it to protect the mail and himself from encounters with robbers and sloth bears!"

Now I saw that, in addition to tea and biscuits, the table

held Father Autry's mail. This was the mailman who brought a satchel of letters for Father Autry from Nepalganj once a month. Father-*sahib* loved his letters. Much of his family lived far away, in the United States, so he made every delivery a celebration with tea and cakes.

Father Autry had retired from teaching, but he was still working, pursuing his dream of being a full-time naturalist. I was his assistant. His brain already held the names of every living thing in the Borderlands, maybe in all of Nepal. I supplied him with our local names for the "flora and fauna," as he liked to call it. I also taught him what I knew about my faith. As a religious man, Father Autry was interested in the different ways to worship a holy spirit.

I nodded hello to the mailman. He slowly blinked his thickly lashed, almond eyes as his reply. Tharus are generally talkative, but it was clear that this man was not. I was excited that here, in my own village, there were still things I didn't know—like this mailman. The jungle was not the only place for discovery.

I asked him in Tharu, "Have you needed your spear lately?"

The mailman smiled. He took a slow sip of tea, then answered. "No. I meet few wild animals these days. But it keeps me clear of human trouble, too."

I laughed and translated for Father Autry, who hadn't seemed to quite understand the man's Tharu dialect. Then the mailman stood ramrod straight like a rosewood tree. He could not stay long, with so many people waiting for their monthly mail delivery. I watched his long, wrinkled fingers grip the heavy spear, lifting it from its resting spot against the wall. I could tell he was still a man of considerable strength—no matter his age or thinness. We bid one another farewell.

"Nandu, look!" my teacher said, holding up a thick journal with a yellow rectangular border. It was the latest issue of *National Geographic*. We read several articles aloud every month as part of our study. Father Autry said that reading this magazine as a boy was how he started on his journey to becoming a naturalist.

As he took a closer look at the magazine's cover, his face changed from a glow to a deep frown.

"What is it, Father-*sahib*?"

"Maybe we should save this for another time."

"Why?"

"Nandu, I think we should . . ."

Before he could finish his sentence, I picked up the magazine he had placed facedown on the table. On the cover was a photograph of an African elephant lying on the ground. Half of the elephant's face was missing—and his tusks were gone. The title on the cover read, *Slaughter of Africa's Wildlife.*

"Nandu, I do not want you to see this," implored Father Autry.

But I was determined to look. I flipped to the story to find picture after picture of dead elephants sprawled on their sides. Some had been shot with high-powered rifles, others with poisoned arrows.

One of the biggest photos in the article was of a dead white rhino. I recognized the square lip, but it was missing both horns. Only bloody stumps remained on the giant's face. I read the caption aloud: "Poachers removed the horns of this white rhino and fled."

The photos on the next pages were smaller but worse. I saw ivory carvers at work, taking the once beautiful tusks of a living elephant and turning them into trinkets. I saw a necklace, a bowl, and even a tiny elephant statue. The caption described them as ornate carvings—all I saw were dead animals. Another photo was of a man shaving rhino horn into a dish for a customer. My hands shook with rage. My stomach grew tight like a drum.

"This is a horrible reality," Father Autry said. "I only wanted to spare you from seeing it."

"Who could be so cruel, Father-*sahib*? And for what purpose?"

"The people who buy ivory are very rich, but it is all decorative, there is no use to it. It only signifies their wealth. But others, who are ill, buy the horn of rhinos because they believe the horns have magical healing powers," said Father Autry.

"They pay a lot of money even though it is nonsense. And the people who live near these wild animals are often very poor. So one horn or one tusk can be a year's salary."

"This poaching would never happen in the Borderlands. We guard our wildlife like our family."

"Nandu, it is always a struggle between humans and the wildlife—"

I interrupted. I hated to, but my mind was racing. "Father Autry, there was this boy that my father and I saw fishing with his father, only they were wearing shoes. I thought something was wrong. And there was. Earlier this morning I caught the boy setting out snares. These people are not from our area, I know it."

"They may have been displaced by the earthquake, Nandu, or the drought has dried up their fields. We never know the plight of another until we ask, or until we have walked a mile in their footsteps."

My face grew hot as I remembered the time I had killed many paradise flycatchers, thinking that it would please Father Autry to send their skins to the Smithsonian Institution in Washington, DC, for research. How foolish I had been to do such a thing. But I hadn't known they were never to be collected, and I had thought I was helping. Still, the shame of that day stayed with me.

"What is it, Nandu?" Father Autry asked, seeing my blazing face.

"I should check on the fawn. I will return tomorrow, and we will visit the Baba as we planned," I said.

"Until tomorrow, then, Nandu," said my tutor quietly, giving me time to think. He knew me well and understood that when I was struggling, I needed to be alone to uncover the truth about my feelings.

On the way back to the stable, my mind raced. If *I* killed beautiful birds, what would stop someone else, someone without a love for animals like mine, an understanding of their intelligence and souls, from killing them to keep from starving? It is easy to miss the truth of what is really happening, especially when the truth is something you do not want to see.

FIVE

B y mid-May, every animal seeks a shady spot from the blistering sun during the day. It is the hottest month of the year, and the absence of any rain made life miserable for all but the brain-fever bird. The males kept calling through the morning. It was only ten o'clock, but after cutting grass with Indra, I was drained from the heat. Even Hira Prashad did not want to leave the cool river when we stopped for him to drink. But if we did not move, we would be late for Father Autry and our meeting with the Baba.

Every region in Nepal has its priest, and we had the Baba. He tended a small temple in the jungle, which he found abandoned while on a long wandering. He lived there, a hermit, in a one-room hut. Every week I brought him firewood. Sometimes Hira Prashad and I would be his only visitors for days. The Baba had declared the forest around his temple off-limits to hunting and trapping. The villagers obeyed the law of the Baba.

Hira Prashad banged the end of his trunk against the ground and let out a long low rumble as we neared the tiny whitewashed temple. A large male tiger glided across our path, unconcerned by our presence.

"Nandu, the tiger is in," Father Autry whispered, putting his fingers to his lips for us to be silent. The tiger walked around the clearing, turned to stare at us once, and then vanished into the ravine beyond the temple.

"What a magnificent animal," he said.

We followed the tiger slowly along the trail by the river, the Jogi Khola, or Holy Man's River, as it was called because of the holy men from the temple who drank and bathed in its waters. The tiger slipped into a deep pool under an overhanging fig tree. In these days of intense drought, this was its refuge. Forty feet down from the tiger was the Baba, lounging in another pool, waving to us and pointing, indicating we should meet him at his temple.

The Baba entered his hut next to the temple to change his robe. He came to greet us with easy simplicity, the same manner in which he had just held his visit with the tiger. The Baba was ancient. He was dressed in his normal saffron robes, and his hennaed hair and beard were unshorn. What was most unusual about him was his friendship with the tiger.

Perhaps because of the law that no one could disturb nature around the temple, this enormous tiger had joined the Baba. They lived peaceably together and formed a friendship of kindred spirits—even though the Baba was as frail as a wood splinter and the tiger had shoulders broader than a man's.

The Baba walked in his careful way toward us, a beaming smile on his face. Ever since the Baba had taken a vow of silence, his eyes glowed brighter, his gestures more comical or gentle, depending on the situation.

"Good afternoon, my friend," said Father Autry.

"Hel-lo, Ba-ba," I sang, a greeting he particularly liked.

The Baba touched his chest with all ten fingers and bowed his head, receiving our greetings. Then he fanned his fingers away from his chest to greet us in return. He invited us to sit on the benches outside his hut, then he went inside, returning a few moments later with teacups. Father Autry spoke in Nepali and the Baba responded with gestures, nodding, and by raising and lowering his eyebrows. More than a year ago, about three months after he had taken up residence in this jungle temple, the Baba had given his voice to Krishna as a sign of devotion. When gestures failed them, they picked up pieces of chalk and wrote to each other in Devanagari script on the writing tablet Father Autry had brought.

I poured the boiling water into the Baba's blue ceramic teapot. I watched the tea leaves swirl and sink into the darkening water. Finally, I found the courage to speak with the two men I trusted like my own father.

"I hope you both will not mind my asking you a serious question," I began.

42

"Of course not, Nandu," said Father Autry. The Baba gestured with his hands moving from me to his chest, so I continued.

"As Father-*sahib* knows, yesterday Indra and I rescued a spotted deer fawn, only two months old, from a snare set by a boy in the forest. We arrived just in time to free the fawn before it was killed. We found fifteen other snares he had set, too."

The Baba held up his hand to tell us to wait. He tiptoed off in his funny gait and went behind his hut. He returned with five wire snares. They were like the ones I had found.

"Where did you find these, Baba?"

He took a stick and drew their locations in the sand. The snares had been set around the temple and in his sanctuary. He made a gesture with his fingers of the tiger walking through the area and put his hand to his heart, fearing the tiger would be snared.

"I will search all over when we are done with tea, Baba, and I will tell *Subba-sahib*. He will speak to the new warden."

"Nandu, tell the Baba what happened to the boy that was setting the snares," said my tutor.

"I warned him never to return."

"You did the right thing. He was probably a village boy trying to feed his family."

I looked down. I never believed this excuse. We rarely eat meat at the stable. What did the villagers need with a fawn?

"Nandu, I can see how upset you are. But you did what we

43

call 'turning the other cheek.' Showing kindness gives people a chance to change."

The Baba nodded his head vigorously. He touched his finger in some ashes and pressed it to my forehead to offer his blessing.

I so basked in their praise I could not bring myself to ask the question that I had wanted to ask. How do you stop people from poaching? How do you stir in others the love for animals that we three shared so deeply? I didn't see how turning the other cheek would work at all. I could not bear to tell them that I had scared the boy with a stick. But I was not sorry. That is what I felt in my heart.

Sometimes religion gets in the way of doing what is needed, I thought. Religious activity—the prayers of Father Autry, the silent chanting of my Hindu Baba, or even the sacrifices to Ban Devi made by my father the shaman—cannot help you find and pick up snares. That was my thought as I left them and set to work. I checked for traps, looking carefully under fruiting trees and where the grass was lush. This boy was smart. I only found one more snare, this one large enough to catch a deer but probably not a tiger.

After I had calmed the Baba's fears about the snares, Father Autry and I rode away on Hira Prashad into the jungle, the Baba waving, as he always did, until we were out of sight.

On the way to Father Autry's bungalow, we must have disturbed a small swarm of horseflies along the trail. At least *they* seemed to be thriving in the drought. "Nandu," Father Autry said, "I believe we have a special subject for today's lesson, which we can have on the back of an elephant."

Lessons with my tutor transported me to another world. Each of Father Autry's teachings pulled another thin veil away from my jungle view. The more I learned, the clearer my vision became.

The horseflies zoomed around us and landed while I rushed to cut branches to swat at them. Horseflies, which often bite me and my elephant, were not what I would have chosen as the subject of today's talk. When I was about to swing my branch at them, Father Autry held me back. "Wait, Nandu, the cavalry has arrived."

From nowhere, several flies—even larger than the horseflies—snatched them from the air. "Behold, Nandu. Meet the robber fly." I had never seen a robber fly. I did not know they even existed! I was always too busy whacking at the horseflies to notice their predator, the robber kind.

Nature keeps the balance, even among the flies. The patient observer will find the balance. That is what Father Autry taught me today: to stop and notice. I would share this new knowledge with Dilly and Rita the next time a horsefly bit into them.

Speaking of insects . . . I returned to camp after my lesson and spotted the new game warden walking into the gazebo followed by a taller man who I did not know. The warden was the chief government officer in the Borderlands, reporting only to the forest conservator for western Nepal. We relied on the warden as the voice of the Borderlands to the conservator. He was very important to us—and to all the wildlife in the jungle.

That man's name was Mr. Dhungel, our new warden. He was a small man in his fifties. His hair was dyed jet black, the same color of a dung beetle. He wore thick black glasses that slipped down his nose. The warden sat with my father in the gazebo, drinking black pepper tea, the kind we serve to special guests—the kind that makes me want to spit. The other man stood rather than sit in a chair.

I bowed, with a *namaste* gesture to the warden. My father had told me that a new man had been assigned to the Borderlands to replace the old warden, Mr. Joshi, who had been transferred to another district. The old warden who did nothing when the Maroons, the outlaws in the Borderlands, terrorized our villages.

"Nandu, please meet our new game warden, Mr. Dhungel. He brings us important news from Birganj. And I have not been introduced to your colleague yet," my father said, nodding to the taller man standing behind the warden.

Dhungel, dung beetle, all the same to me.

"*Subba-sahib*, this is Ganesh Lal," said Mr. Dhungel. "He has just joined our staff. He will be assisting me. He knows a

46

lot about the wildlife. He comes from a hunting family in the hills."

Ganesh Lal nodded to us and gave me a half smile.

I bowed again to the new warden and his game scout.

"*Subba-sahib*, I have some news about the Baba and his tiger."

"Nandu, I will first share the warden's news. Sit."

This sounded ominous.

"I do not think there is cause for concern," my father began. "Dhungel-*sahib* says that Birganj was hit hard by the earthquake. Several buildings collapsed. The police were needed for the search-and-rescue, and the jail was left guarded by a single janitor." My father paused here to look me closely in the eye. "Someone entered the jail, Nandu. He knocked the janitor unconscious, and released the prisoners."

"Did they find them?" I asked.

"Yes, Nandu, most of them were caught," Mr. Dhungel answered. "But two got away. They were Maroons. They were last seen on a freight train headed to India."

"Why were we not told sooner?" Fear gripped at my throat. "It has been more than a week since the earthquake!"

The warden looked at me and swept the thumb and forefinger of both hands in the air. That is our national gesture that means something like, *What can I do?*

"But we captured the Maroons!" I said, my voice rising. "They will come back for revenge. *Subba-sahib*, what if they try to burn down the stable?"

47

I could not believe such bad luck. Maybe the old drivers were right. Maybe the earthquake was a terrible sign of things to come.

Subba-sahib raised his hand to calm me. "Nandu has had a bad experience with the Maroons," he explained to the warden. *Subba-sahib* went on to tell the warden of my discovery of the Maroons' hideout, the terror Kalomutu and his gang had inflicted on the Borderlands, and my run-in with the Maroons on the road to Gularia.

My father then turned to me. "Nandu, there is good news, too. Kalomutu is in prison in Kathmandu," he said. "His sentence has been handed down by the high court. For robbing so many villages in the Borderlands and killing several people, he will spend the rest of his life behind bars."

My father read the concern in my eyes.

I did not believe this was the last we would see of the Maroons. I saw the face of the Maroon I shot with my slingshot. The men who escaped would return—to find me.

SIX

The hind end of a baby rhino stuck out of the cookhouse door. I was not sure if it was Ritu or Rona waiting for her morning bottle of milk. I walked toward the cookhouse to visit the Ancient Babies and play with the fawn, Nani.

"Ritu and Rona get fed first or there will be trouble," Rita cooed to the tiny deer as she held a bottle in each hand for the rhinos. "And we do not want trouble from these big babies," she whispered.

"Rita, I can help," I said. I took a third bottle from the stove and offered it to Nani, but she backed away and hid between Rita's legs. Rita was so tall and thin there was not much to hide behind.

"She has already found a new mother," I said.

Rita laughed. "She is perfect, no? But I love you two girls, too," she added, looking at her rhinos, who had finished their breakfast. She put their bottles aside and took the third one from me to feed Nani. The rhinos bleated at her, begging for more milk, but she pushed them out of the cookhouse. They galloped over to the shade of a *kadam* tree and plopped down below it, ready to nap. The fawn joined them once she had finished her bottle, sprawling out next to Rona.

"They have become such good friends so quickly!" Rita exclaimed, proud of her brood.

"I must bring Father Autry by to see them," I told her. "He will want pictures of this."

"Oh, yes, he will!" agreed Rita. She suddenly grew serious. "Nandu, we are running so low on powdered milk for Rona and Ritu. Do you think *Subba-sahib* can send for more from the bazaar? I checked at the teahouse in Thakurdwara. They were completely out."

"No need. I will take Dilly's bike to the next village. They will have some."

But when I got to the village beyond Thakurdwara, they were out, too. I kept going farther and farther, to the next village, then the next. By the time I was done, I was halfway to the Indian border. The powdered milk we wanted was nowhere to be found. I returned at midday to tell my father.

"We must send someone across the border to the bazaar at Bichia to purchase a month's supply," he said. "Right now, I need everyone here to prepare for the arrival of the new elephants."

"*Subba-sahib*, I can ask Father Autry. He said he wanted to make a supply run this week. Maybe he can move his trip up two days."

I walked to Father Autry's bungalow and found him on his veranda, deep in a book about praying mantids and walking sticks. In ten minutes, we were in his Land Rover and on our way to India. An hour later we approached the border checkpoint. Father Autry's driver, Dhan Bahadur, would stay with the car on the Nepal side, because my tutor did not have the proper permit to bring his vehicle across the border. We would have to cross on foot to the town of Bichia.

Bichia means *scorpion* in Hindi, and this border town was full of them. The brown scorpion has a sting that burns like fire. The black scorpion's sting feels more like a bee's. *Bichia* is also slang for pickpockets, who were as common here as the scorpions.

Bicycle rickshaw drivers honked at us offering a ride. "Come, Nandu, let's walk. It will do me good," said Father Autry.

"This heat can kill an American," I warned, half-jokingly. There was no stopping Father Autry, though.

Father's Autry's face did turn a shade pinker on the walk to the market. He wiped a lot of sweat from his forehead as we ordered twenty-four boxes of milk formula at a small stall. Next to us, a man was placing an order at the same time. He could not suppress his smile as he looked at Father Autry and me. "A

Jesuit and a Tibetan. That is a pairing we do not see around here much. And hoarding so much milk formula, one would think you were feeding an orphanage."

We all laughed at our peculiar circumstances. I liked that the man immediately understood my heritage, even though I knew so little about it myself. I was proud to be called a Tibetan.

"Not quite, sir," I said. "The milk is for the baby rhinos we are raising in our camp. They *are* orphans, though."

We introduced ourselves properly then while the shop owner climbed up a ladder to reach the boxes of formula. "It is an honor to meet you both. I am Dr. Aziz, the local physician here in Bichia. Welcome, friends," he said. "Please tell me more about your unusual orphans."

I told Dr. Aziz how we called them the Ancient Babies because they looked so prehistoric but that they nursed from a baby bottle. I also told him about Nani and the new baby elephants we were expecting soon. Dr. Aziz laughed at the image of so many babies under our care. "I should like to come to your stable and see these young animals for myself one day."

"You would be most welcome, Dr. Aziz," Father Autry said.

"And may I offer you an invitation to share a meal next time you are in Bichia?"

Father Autry and I each most heartily accepted. It was such a good feeling of friendship. We waved good-bye and headed to the square to look for a bicycle rickshaw to transport our supplies back to the border.

At the edge of the wooden stalls, vegetable and fruit sellers squatted on the dusty ground, their produce laid out before them on sheets. The greens and cucumbers had wilted in the heat. Down the alley were other traders, selling knives, pots, pans, and tools. Off to the side, I heard a familiar grating voice call "Nandooo. . . ."

I recognized him at once with his long, crooked nose and dirty fingernails. It was the peddler they called the Birdman, who sold parakeets and talking mynahs and any other bird he could catch or kill. He was a regular in the Gularia bazaar in the Borderlands. Arranged in front of the Birdman were the casques of hornbills and a few barking deer antlers. He had several live birds for sale as well.

"What are you doing in Bichia, Birdman?" I asked.

"Ah, young elephant driver. The drought is even worse in the Borderlands than here in India. None of the wild parakeets laid eggs this year. This drought will ruin my business. Look, I only have a few birds here. Will you buy a very smart mynah?" The mynah looked woozy and miserable from the heat. So did the Birdman. I looked closely at his sunken cheeks and wrinkled face. The drought was sucking him dry.

Other peddlers began shouting at us. "Come buy our treasures! Drink from this bottle, you will live to be ninety! Chew this bark every day for strong teeth!" I guided Father Autry along and whispered, "Do not make eye contact, Father-*sahib*, it only encourages them." He dropped his gaze to the dusty road. We were nearly out of the open area when a dark-skinned man with a long moustache ran up to us and tugged on Father Autry's sleeve. The peddler quickly pulled out a velvet satchel with bracelets and necklaces of stones. My tutor shook his head no. The man whispered, "Special carvings. For holy man, I have a good price."

He held up a handful of small carved rhinos for Father Autry to see. From a pocket, he pulled two ivory-colored necklaces. "Feel them," he said. "They are beautiful."

They were not beautiful. They were made from ivory. Elephant tusk ivory.

I followed, angry, after Father Autry. "Why do people treat animals like objects to trade?" I asked. "Why kill an elephant to make silly necklaces and stupid carvings?"

"I know, Nandu. It looks like he is not having much luck. And what he is doing is not legal. At least no elephants in the Borderlands have been poached in some time."

I wanted to remind him that this was almost not true. The Python would have made off with Hira Prashad's tusks had Dilly and I not stopped him. But I said nothing. Three more men approached, one trying to sell us his pet rhesus monkey and another holding scorpions in his palm and offering them as powerful medicine. The mascot of Bichia. I wanted to get away as fast as I could.

Up ahead in the open field, a crowd of villagers had formed a circle. People were laughing and cheering. We waded into the crowd to see what was causing the ruckus. A wiry man dressed in a blue shirt and red-and-gold-striped trousers was singing to a sloth bear. The bear was wearing a chain collar attached to a heavy weight to keep him from lunging at anyone. When the man shouted, "Dance, my talented bear!" the bear stood up on his hind legs and shuffled this way and that. "Smile, smile, my friend! Your adoring fans will throw money at you!"

The bear broke into a grin that broke my heart. This was so humiliating. I wanted to rush in and free the bear.

My sadness gave way to rage, but Father Autry pulled me away before I could act. "Come, Nandu, let's leave this awful scene behind and bring the milk formula for your Ancient Babies. We don't want them to go hungry tonight."

In an hour we were bundled into a rickshaw and headed back to the border and then home. Father Autry insisted on paying for the rhinos' formula, and now we had two months' worth.

"Thank you, Father-*sahib*," I said. "I only hope my father will accept your kindness. We have little money to feed our growing orphanage."

Silence filled the Land Rover on our trip home. I thought about my own behavior when I threatened the boy in the jungle. I regretted it now. Maybe that is how these peddlers of animal parts got started. Someone was very cruel to them as young children. How else could they grow up to make a living causing such suffering to animals?

"Father-*sahib*?" I ventured.

"Yes, Nandu."

"I would like to make a confession." I had heard that Catholics speak to their priests in this way.

"Carry on, then, Nandu, if you feel the need."

"That boy who had caught the spotted deer fawn in the snare? I did not turn the other cheek. Before I warned him never to return to the Borderlands and let him go, I threatened to beat him with a stick."

"I see."

"I apologize for lying to you and the Baba. I should have told the truth."

"Well, you did now, and that is what counts. And, to be completely honest, if I were in your place, I might have been tempted to give him a good thwack myself."

I smiled.

Then my tutor grew serious. "But now, I hope you see that such retaliations come from the same place that drives people to do wrong. The boy hurt the fawn, and you threatened to hurt him. We can only hope to make a real difference by meeting ugliness with goodness."

I stayed silent, but inside I was not sure it was this simple. Even if I had hit that boy, he would have been back setting snares the next day.

Father Autry continued, "I look forward to meeting this

lucky fawn. Remember, you saved her life, too. That is something to be proud of, Nandu."

Father Autry's words lifted my spirits, as they often do. I had not slept well since the news of the Maroons' escape, but that night I dreamed of riding Hira Prashad across the Great Sand Bar River to meet Devi Kali, our mother, to tell her we are doing fine. And that we miss her.

We miss her. . . .

SEVEN

had felt like an ant amidst the human crush in the Bichia bazaar. That feeling evaporated the moment I rode Hira Prashad into the great grassland across the Belgadi River. In a patch of green grass, one of the few left, I saw the mayor, Pradhan, tending his females. I preferred this mayor to any human one in any town. I realized I would not last a week in Bichia. There had to be a reason why my parents left me in a jungle rather than abandon me in an Indian border town. They must have known something about what was inside me, waiting to come out when I grew up, my love of this wildness all around me.

Hira Prashad moved across the grassland and grabbed handfuls of wild sugarcane wherever he could find it still green. Everything was drying up. We had been out most of the day and I realized I had finished all the water in my canteen over two hours ago. My throat was parched, and my voice was raspy.

"Look, Hira Prashad, there is an *amala* tree," I said. I steered him next to a spindly tree in the middle of the grassland. I grabbed some of the ripe hard green fruits from the leafless branches. I remembered my father's words to me when we had been out all day in the hot sun: "Suck on these, Nandu, when you are without water to drink and deep in the jungle. Take the *amala* fruit. Its sour taste will quench your thirst."

I popped three in my mouth at one time. I had forgotten how sour the fruit was! My craving for water was gone, though. I loved how the jungle provided all that we needed.

Even though it was an hour before sunset it was still terribly hot. I turned Hira Prashad toward the Belgadi so he could drink his fill. We came upon rhesus monkeys near the river; they seemed too exhausted to notice us. Near the banks of the Belgadi, gray langur monkeys were licking the salt from the rocks in the receding riverbed. A blue bull bent low to drink from one of the last pools of water in the river, which was now flowing like a trickle.

A flash of silver caught my eye and then more. I steered my tusker closer and saw them: a whole school of fish trapped in a puddle only a few inches deep. In this drought, the puddle would dry out by tomorrow and they would all die if a mongoose or otter did not eat them first. The *National Geographic* images, and the man with the moustache selling the elephant ivory popped back into my head. I jumped off my tusker and tried scooping the fish out of the puddle and into the main channel, where they could swim away from danger. But they were hard to catch in my cupped hands and there were hundreds. I would be at it all night at the meager rate I was capturing them and carrying them to the main channel.

I called Hira Prashad and told him to dig with his trunk. *"Kun, Kun!"* I shouted, digging with him to show what I wanted. In fifteen minutes we had dug a deep trench and it began to fill with water. Some of the fish shot off into the main stream but others still lingered. I went to the end of the puddle and shuffled my bare feet to herd the fish out of the eddy. They were free.

I mounted my elephant and we headed to the edge of the forest two miles south of the crossing to our camp. Here the rosewoods were thick and the young saplings had been bent in all directions, trampled by hungry rhinos. It was their favorite food. Three rhinos trotted across the floodplain, alarmed by our approach. I loved to watch them canter, making huffing noises with each step of their funny three-toed feet. It was time to head back to camp.

We crossed the Belgadi River south of the stable, where the river borders the outskirts of Thakurdwara. At the edge of the trees, the village fields began, or what was left of them. In a normal year, the maize would be a foot high, but we passed only fields full of withered stalks. The lentil crop had vanished. Only where the Tharu farmers had dug an irrigation canal bringing water from the Belgadi River to their fields was there a narrow ribbon of green rice paddies slicing through the brown landscape.

I heard a noise like a rhino about to attack. It was only the *Budghar*, the village headman in the seat of his tractor, the only one in the Borderlands. Perched on the wheel well was his eldest son, Hala Ram. They both waved. The *Budghar* shut off the tractor and they walked over to me.

Last year, Dilly and I had been riding back from the Gularia market in the oxcarts belonging to the *Budghar* and Hala Ram and his uncle. We were held up on the way by a gang of Maroons who almost killed Hala Ram. My friend was struck by a dagger thrown by a Maroon with a beard. I shot the robber in the head with my slingshot and he fell from his horse. I rushed Hala Ram back to the health post in Gularia. Thankfully, he survived. The robber did not.

The *Budghar* smiled broadly at me. I was his favorite, ever since we saved his son's life. He was a big man, who put clarified butter on his rice, something no one else could afford. It is said that he ate one duck or chicken at every meal. That made him the heaviest person in the Borderlands.

"*Ram, Ram*, Nandu. Why are you out in this cursed heat wave?"

I told him about being in Bichia and needing to clear my head.

"You didn't run into any more Maroons along the way

there, did you?" He laughed. I told him what Mr. Dhungel had told us about the leader of the group and the rest of the gang. "Good riddance to them." He spat on the ground.

The *Budghar* swept his meaty arm across the barren fields. "The gods are very angry with us, Nandu. First the earthquake and now this drought. Can *Subba-sahib* talk to Ban Devi and make it rain?"

"I will make inquiries, *Budghar-sahib*," and then we all broke into laughter with a bitter edge. What else could we do? The drought would end when it would end. We had to endure.

EIGHT

Do you know how if you bring an umbrella with you it never rains, and when you forget one, you get drenched in a downpour? We tried that trick, too. Drivers always carry umbrellas to shield them from the sun or the rain. Ramji, our anti-shaman, said around the campfire the other night, "Maybe if we forget our umbrellas when we take the elephants out to graze, it will be looked on as a sign to the gods and the June rains will start." We decided to give it a try.

I thought Ramji's reverse advice was working immediately. Gray clouds drifted into camp. But within a few minutes, I realized it was just haze. Smoke from a grassland fire had settled over the stable. We were still in the grip of the worst drought in a century. That is what they said on the radio. How they knew this exactly, I did not know.

Please, Ban Devi, let it rain.

Indra took Hira Prashad out to graze while I helped Rita

store the boxes of powdered milk Father Autry and I had brought back from Bichia. There was hardly enough room on the shelves to hold them all. My father stood by with a cup of tea in his hand.

"Nandu, you should have not let Father Autry pay for the milk supplies," he said.

"He refused to let me pay one penny for it, *Subba-sahib*."

"We must find a way to thank him, then."

Just then Indra came across the sparse grass in the open area of camp. "*Subba-sahib*, Nandu!"

Indra was so upset the words barely came out.

"Pradhan," he said, his voice cracking.

"What is it, Indra?"

"Pradhan is dead, *Subba-sahib*. Shot in the great grassland. They took his horn!"

Anger and shock hung like a storm cloud over the line of six elephants marching to Pradhan's body. *Subba-sahib* and Mr. Dhungel were at the lead followed by Ganesh Lal, the game scout. The inquest into Pradhan's death would be a serious investigation—more serious than if a person had been killed. Rhinos were property of the king. To steal a rhino's horn was to steal from King Birendra himself.

Vultures circled and swarmed in the sky—an eerie marker of our destination. Vultures or no, it was hard to miss Pradhan lying on his side in the trampled, bloody grass. His armored plates were cut and scarred from recent fights. Wounds that would never heal. The great Pradhan, mayor of the Borderlands, had died at the small hands of men. Tears sprang to my eyes at the sight of my old friend Pradhan. Murdered.

I stifled the scream that choked my throat.

My father climbed off his elephant and knelt down next to Pradhan's face to examine the bullet holes. "Two shots fired into the skull from close range," he said to the warden. He turned his body toward the grass thicket nearby. "The poachers must have crawled on their bellies to get this close," he added. "I see no footprints."

Mr. Dhungel was busy filling out his official forms, which would be sent directly to the king's secretary. "*Subba-sahib*, I am writing that this male was very old," said the warden. "That is what I will put in my report. And you will confirm this. He probably would not have lived out the year anyway."

But no excuse could cover up the bullet holes or replace the stolen horn. My father replied with a clear fact: "A horn of that size is worth three million rupees, Warden-*sahib*."

Dhungel-*sahib* winced. Ganesh Lal stared at the ground.

When the call was given by the warden, the men lifted their *kukhris*, the sharp knife every Nepali man carries, over their heads. They were required by law to send the hooves and the skin to Kathmandu. The horn, which was normally sent to the Royal Palace, was probably somewhere in India by now.

I could not bear to look. Who can watch this happen to a member of your family?

I joined *Subba-sahib* on the ground, where he was tracking the criminals' path. I had to continually will myself not to cry in front of the other drivers.

"*Subba-sahib*, when the warden and Ganesh Lal are done, can we bury Pradhan here, in his own kingdom?"

"Yes, Nandu, but first let us try to find out more from these tracks. Look here." He pointed. There were human footprints on the dirt track that led to the Great Sand Bar River. "And look here." The barefoot prints changed to shoeprints. "They put down their load and put on their shoes."

We followed the shoeprints along the trail heading toward the river.

Then we saw the footprint of a large male tiger merging onto the dirt track and behind the human footprints. "Look. They ran here. Two of them. They must have seen the tiger."

I scanned the area ahead of us while my father bent close to the ground. He was a skilled tracker, with an elephant's sixth sense of what tracks tell us.

A few feet up the dirt trail, one set of tracks changed. "Ah, one of his shoes fell off running from the tiger," my father said.

In the bushes, I saw a burst of color against the dull, dry leaves. It was blue. A blue canvas sneaker.

I crumpled to the ground. My chest heaved without getting any air. My father knelt down and placed his arm across my shoulders to steady me. "We will catch them, Nandu. We will catch them."

I could not tell my father about my agony. Pradhan was dead because of me. I had threatened the boy. This was his retribution. My anger, my stupidity, had killed one of the greatest creatures to ever live.

PART II
ARRIVALS

NINE

ona and Ritu dipped their lips into my vest pockets. They knew where to find the dried sugarcane pieces I had hidden away. Our Ancient Babies curled the treats into their mouths, smacking their lips with joy. I rubbed my hands over their thick warm skin. I kept rubbing and they kept leaning into me for more. The young rhinos made the loss of Pradhan easier to bear. If only slightly.

"Nandu, remember these may be Pradhan's daughters," *Subba-sahib* said. "And let us concentrate on the arrivals of the elephant calves. Come, I need you to help me lay out where we will tether the new elephants to their poles." *Subba-sahib* was right. He always was. The new elephant calves were the reason our lives could continue at the stable. They were our hope.

The morning finally came, on June 15, when we met the elephant drivers from Kanchanpur at the banks of the Great

Sand Bar River. The drivers, with four mother elephants and their calves, were waiting on the other side of the river when we arrived. It had been a long three-day walk from their stable in western Nepal.

From the back of Hira Prashad, Rita and I waved to the drivers. They returned our greeting with wildly flailing arms. The river between us was low and would not start rising until the snow melted in the Himalayas.

"Why don't they let the mothers and calves swim across?" Rita asked.

"There is a deep part, in the middle, that is over the calves' heads. *Subba-sahib* does not want to take the risk," I said. Instead, a barge would carry the new elephants across the open water. Through my binoculars, I could clearly see the drivers from Kanchanpur guiding the four adult females onto the boat.

"Look, Rita, the mothers are herding their calves onto the barge!" I said.

Their ears flared while they gently swept the babies on board with their trunks. I thought of Devi Kali then and what a mother she had been to me. I rubbed the top of Hira Prashad's head, knowing he might be thinking of her, too.

Behind me, Rita would not stop fidgeting. I was used to her restlessness when we went out into the jungle, but today it annoyed me.

"Let me look, Nandu!" she said. I scanned the whole length

of the river, taking my time, before I handed the binoculars to her. I was looking for the old female elephant I had seen just before the earthquake. But she was not there.

Everyone watched closely, in silence, as the bargemen slowly poled the four elephants, three calves, and their drivers across the river. At one point, the raft tipped, and a mother scrambled a bit. Another of the elephants let out a soft trumpet.

The barge slid onto the sandy bank on our side. We cheered and our elephants rumbled. Our new arrivals carefully disembarked, the mothers keeping their calves close to them.

Subba-sahib barked out his orders to us. "Ten elephants from our stable into two lines of five each. I will lead one side on Bhim Prashad. Nandu, you lead the other on your tusker." In between we put Punti Kali, the pregnant twenty-year-old, who walked next to Hira Prashad, followed by the three females with their calves.

"Drivers from Kanchanpur, stay close to your assigned calf. Drivers on elephants, be on the lookout for tigers. They will take a straggler calf, so we must not take our eyes off them."

Our caravan traveled slowly, adjusting to the pace of the exhausted calves. We stopped twice when one or the other dropped to the ground for a short nap. It would take us more than four hours to cover the same distance that our older elephants could do in thirty minutes.

"These poor little jumbos, they cannot walk much more

today," said Rita. As we traveled, the elephants never stopped rumbling. I imagined they had a lot to talk about.

We entered the giant grassland before the Belgadi. It was here where we used to see Pradhan grazing and tending his three female rhinos. They were here still, but Pradhan was not. In his place was another large male rhino.

"Pradhan's rival has taken over, Rita." The male rhino faced us and snorted loudly. He probably had never seen so many elephants before. I wished that Pradhan would have been replaced the natural way, by losing a fight and being pushed out of his territory. That would have been honorable, the way of the jungle. And even though I would not have seen Pradhan after his loss, I would know that he was still alive until he met his natural death.

The roars, whistles, moans, and rumbles from the fifteen elephants left behind greeted us as we came closer to the stable. They were as excited as we were for the new arrivals. Chained to their tethering posts, they raised their trunks to inhale the scent of the newcomers. We crossed under the marigold-covered arch over the gate at the entrance to the stable. The noise from all the elephants was deafening.

"Nandu," said Rita, "our elephants are saying hello."

Even the tired calves had begun squeaking to the others . . . squeaking, I hoped, with delight. But was this a good life to be born into? For the first time, I saw the tethering chains on the waiting elephants like the chains on prisoners. But these elephants were not criminals. They were part of our family. Yet still, there were chains. Was this the life these baby calves deserved? My cheeks grew hot, and I felt the anguish I had felt seeing Pradhan's lifeless body. I did not know what to think.

After our entire breeding center staff gathered round, *Subba-sahib* welcomed the head of the Kanchanpur stable. Tonight would be a small feast, washed down with lots of *raksi*. The new conservator-*sahib* would arrive tomorrow for the formal ceremony and inspection. Everything needed to be perfect for his report to the royal palace.

The new females were led to their tethering posts flanking Prem Kali. *Subba-sahib* wanted them to feel safe under the watch of the oldest and wisest female in our stable. Once the mothers were secured with their calves nearby, my father walked over to us. Rita and I were still atop Hira Prashad, who had not stopped rumbling to the new elephants. I wished he could tell me how they felt about their new home.

"Rita, you will have to keep the rhino calves away from the little elephants for a few days. If they come too close, the mothers may panic and charge them."

Rita's face grew downcast. She could not hide any emotion. She loved taking care of Ritu and Rona and now Nani the spotted deer fawn. They followed her everywhere. But she also wanted to be the leader in caring for the new elephants.

Subba-sahib sensed her disappointment. "Tomorrow morning, after you feed the rhino calves and Nani, you can help the new drivers brush and bathe the baby elephants."

In an instant, her face was lit up like the sun. If we hadn't been riding Hira Prashad, I think she would have started turning cartwheels.

"Thank you, *Subba-sahib!*"

Dilly had finished making *kuchis* for Mel Kali, and Indra had done the same for Hira Prashad. *Kuchis* were what kept the elephants wanting to return to the stable every night: a packet holding a meal of unhusked rice, rock salt, and hardened molasses wrapped in elephant grass.

We left my elephant, and then the four of us backed fifty feet away from the babies and their mothers so we could watch them. The babies lifted their trunks and squealed in our direction. "Dilly," I said. "We will have to hold Rita back or she will be over there in a flash." Rita threw a *kuchi* at me.

"I will hug them tomorrow," she declared.

We stayed until it grew dark and they had finished nursing. Then the young calves one by one dropped to the ground for a sound night's sleep.

"Look how they snuggle next to their mothers," she said. "So safe in their new home." I looked at Rita's face and her eyes were tearing up. We could not wait for tomorrow morning.

I woke several times to check on the elephants from the front porch of the barracks. Elephants hardly need much sleep, only about four hours each night. But all three times I checked, the other elephants were lying on their sides and breathing deeply. Only one was standing. Hira Prashad's tusks gleamed in the light of the waning moon as he stood guard over his herd.

I was proud of my tusker.

TEN

The *mahouts*, single file, led the elephants to the river. They entered the forest that hung at the edge of camp like a green velvet curtain. A few hours of rain had given us hope that our fortune was changing and the monsoon would arrive on time. Even a short downpour had made the trees around camp, barren until now, send out new leaves. But it was just a temporary relief. We were still in the thick of the drought. We had to make sure the tiny elephant calves drank lots of water.

Indra, my *mahout*, urged Hira Prashad to move out with the herd, but he refused to budge. I walked up and shouted *"Agat! Agat!"* but he did not listen to me, either. Still chained to their poles were Punti Kali and the three mothers and their calves. It was no use. Our tusker would not leave their side, choosing hunger rather than desertion of the new elephants. The other drivers would bring back the grass fodder for the new arrivals. Now they would have to cut fodder for our tusker, too.

Indra looked back at *Subba-sahib* and me and shrugged as if to say, *What can I do?*

My father chuckled. I think he was happy to see Hira Prashad's protectiveness.

"Hira Prashad is ready to adopt every calf that arrives," I said proudly.

"He has the character of a great leader," my father said. "And I want to let him lead. I also need to maintain the routine of the stable. It is a difficult path to walk, Nandu, being in charge of the fate of spirits greater than your own."

I wanted to ask my father if being in charge of those spirits was right. Did Ban Devi approve? But this was not the time to ask such questions. "Do you think the mothers feel safe enough?"

"Yes, life in a stable is what they know, but we must gradually introduce the newcomers to our schedule," he continued. "You must trust me on this."

"Of course, *Subba-sahib*," I said.

Tulsi had spent the morning in the kitchen, preparing a feast for the arrival of the new conservator-*sahib*. Father Autry had sent over three chickens and several ducks for the meal. The Baba would join us, too, though he drank only the tea he brought himself. He never ate meat.

By two in the afternoon, it was time to bathe the elephants, before our guests arrived. It would be the first chance we had to get close to the new calves.

Baghu, the *Subba-sahib* from Kanchanpur, introduced us to our youngest arrivals, as the elephants got lined up for the walk to the river. "The one with the longest trunk and big head is Laxmi Kali. She is the most mischievous. If there is trouble to look for in the stable she will find it first. Keep her out of the cookhouse. She will knock things over. And when you are fixing *kuchis*, be alert. She will try to sneak into the sacks of unhusked rice."

"She is rambunctious and cute. I bet she can get away with anything," said Dilly.

Baghu continued with introductions. "This middle-size one with the long tail is Mina Kali. She is very shy. But watch this." He scratched Mina Kali's chin and she squealed with delight. "That one over there, the smallest calf, is called Shanti Kali. She is curious but very gentle." She was over sniffing the Ancient Babies. Shanti Kali's mother swung her trunk and snorted, telling her baby to take care. But the calf stayed with the rhinos, trying to get them to play.

"Nandu, she seems more interested in our Ancient Babies than with the other two little jumbos." Rita laughed. "That is what we will call all three of them, our little jumbos," she said.

Finally, our little jumbos followed their mothers to the bathing spot, with Hira Prashad taking up the rear. Hira Prashad immediately moved downstream from the calves where he could respond to any danger. He was relishing his role as leader, I could tell. He was always the last one to drag out of the river at bathing time, but now he wasn't even tempted to bathe until the others had finished.

There was no need to worry. The little jumbos were allowed to splash and roll about only in the shallowest eddy, where the water rose barely to their bellies. One of the new drivers started furiously scrubbing Mina Kali with a scrub made from the *loofah*, the dried wild cucumber vine. But soon Shanti Kali was pushing Mina out of the way to have the driver to herself. Their trunks were so clumsy at this age, but they tried to wrap them around his legs. Then Laxmi Kali joined in. Indra and I cooed to them and, with the help of the new drivers, rubbed the young calves with the sponges. Their mothers looked on calmly. Only when the *mahouts* led the three calves out of the water, with the mothers following, did Hira Prashad roll onto his side for his own rubdown. At least this is one benefit our elephants have over their wild relatives.

An hour later, Rita, Dilly, Indra, and I were standing at the gate with the other members of camp, ready to greet the new conservator. I found myself repeating silently, "Let him be better than the last one. Let him be smart and a friend to us and the elephants."

A cloud of dust rose in a thin diagonal line from the road. A car was arriving. It was rare to see a car out here on the western edge of the Borderlands.

How different the new forest conservator-*sahib* was from his predecessor, a heavy man I called Watermelon Belly. This new one stepped out of the jeep and looked like he had left half of himself in the front seat. He was very tall and thin. His bony face protruded from under his *topi*, the small, multicolored cap all Nepali officials wear.

"So, the elephants arrived from Kanchanpur safe and sound?" he asked my father in a pleasant voice. The forest conservator-*sahib*'s name was Mr. Rijal. I liked him better already.

My father and Baghu, the leaders of each stable, stepped forward. Baghu was a gentle, dark-skinned man, even stockier than my father and fifteen years his junior. Baghu nodded his head in the direction of the conservator-*sahib* and made the *namaste* gesture with his hands. My father smiled, but he did not lower his head or bring his hands together, or utter *namaste*. He only bowed before the king and queen. Baghu stepped back to let my father to do the talking.

"Welcome, Conservator-*sahib*. Baghu-*sahib* has brought us three splendid female elephants and their calves from the king's stable. And our pregnant elephant, Punti Kali, looks like she will bear a fine calf in a few months' time. Our breeding center, now stocked with young elephants, is ready for your inspection."

I turned around to see all the drivers lined up in their green uniforms over by the tethering posts. Watching from the fire pit area were our real guests of honor—or at least to me. Father Autry wore a dark sport jacket that contrasted strongly with his pale pink skin and white hair. He was carrying his camera and assorted lenses to document the ceremony. Next to him was the Baba, wrapped in saffron robes. He had dyed his long beard with henna again just for this occasion, and twisted his shoulder-length hair into braids. He had painted his face white and red and wore a necklace of thick red *Rudraksha* seeds typical of *sadhus*. The Hindu ascetic could not have looked more different from the Jesuit priest, but they loved to be in each other's company and converse about the world in chalk on the Baba's tablet. I waved to both of them, and they waved back.

Our new elephants were released from their tethering posts and brought forward. Hira Prashad rumbled loudly. I could see he was not happy about the conservator-*sahib* approaching the calves.

"*Raaa!*" I shouted, and he stopped rumbling immediately.

The conservator-*sahib*, Mr. Rijal, walked up to Mina Kali's mother, whose name was Ratna Kali, and slapped her on the butt. She ignored him. Then he inspected Shanti Kali's mother, Bina Kali, who stood scratching herself with a piece of wood held in her trunk. Punti Kali rumbled deeply enough to make the new official think twice about approaching her. Like my father, these elephants were taking a wait-and-see attitude toward him.

"Come look at these young calves, Conservator-*sahib*," my father said.

"Yes, I am anxious to meet them," he said. "His Majesty

will be pleased with the new center and the elephants."
Mr. Dhungel walked five steps behind his boss, and Ganesh Lal
walked five steps behind the dung beetle, the warden who was
his boss. That is how it is in Nepal. We see rank everywhere, and
must respect it.

Mina and Shanti Kali took a few steps toward the
conservator-*sahib* to reach the tiny *kuchis* he held out for them.
Then Laxmi Kali took one step back and went straight for
Mr. Rijal and head-butted him. He lost his balance and fell to
the ground. I threw my hands over Rita's mouth before she
could let out a laugh. The other drivers looked away or scuffed
the earth with their bare feet to keep from doing the same.

"Charming, yes, but feisty, too, especially this Laxmi Kali,"
said my father as he and Baghu helped Mr. Rijal to his feet. But
rather than berate my father like Watermelon Belly would
have done, the official laughed and brushed off his trousers.

"Now, *Subba-sahib*, how will you manage this increase of
seven elephants? You realize I cannot grant you more funds
from my budget to hire new staff. You must make do with what
you have."

"We will manage, Conservator-*sahib*. Baghu-*sahib* will trans-
fer over ten men to our stable, and he will cover their wages
and ration. For the calves, we have a volunteer to help the drivers look after them."

"A volunteer? This is unusual. And who is this person? Does
he have any special experience tending to young elephants?"

"Rita, step forward!" my father called to her.

I could see her trembling and then, just like that, regain control.

For the first time, the official seemed annoyed. "You assign a young girl to look after two-year-old elephants? *Subba-sahib*, this is an elephant stable, not a school."

I winced, but my father showed not even a flicker of anger.

"Conservator-*sahib*, this is an elephant breeding center, His Majesty's Royal Elephant Breeding Center. And we need someone with the patience and devotion to care for them. Rita has raised our two rhino calves, and they respond to her like puppies. She will do the same for the young elephants. I assure you, she is most capable."

My face flushed with happiness for Rita. Hers must have been on fire when she heard the praise from *Subba-sahib*.

The three calves suddenly rushed over to Rita and began grabbing her closed fists with the tips of their trunks to release the tiny *kuchis*. "As you can see," my father continued, "Mina, Laxmi, and Shanti Kali seem to have made up their minds about her."

"Very well, then, Rita," the conservator-*sahib* said firmly but not unkindly. "The king expects a lot from you. These three calves are national treasures."

Rita bowed deeply. Mr. Rijal turned away and motioned my father to walk with him back to his car. Apparently, he could not stay for the feast and the singing and dancing afterward.

We could not hear what they were saying, but after the jeep roared off, my father returned to us, his face tight and no longer smiling.

"What is it, *Subba-sahib*?" I asked.

"Nandu, Dilly, you see our honored guests standing there, Father-*sahib* and the Baba, and no one has offered them a chair or masala tea. What kind of hosts are we?" We raced to grab chairs for them, and I bowed to both of my friends.

"Thank you, Nandu, but before we sit down the Baba and I are here to perform a very important ceremony—the blessing of the new elephants," said Father Autry.

The Baba nodded, then grabbed his ash pot and filled it from the fire. He mixed it with some colored dyes in sections on his *puja* tray in preparation for making the *tika* marks on the heads of the elephants while he silently prayed for their good health.

I heard Father Autry say to the *sadhu*, "Dear Baba, I am afraid my religion does not have a specific prayer for the blessing of young elephants. I will have to fashion something, I suppose."

The Baba smiled back and gestured that they should start. Two calves were brought forward, Rita walking between them and a hand on each of their backs, stroking them.

They approached the Baba and Father Autry, and Laxmi Kali reached out her trunk and knocked the ash from the Baba's hands. The *sadhu* laughed silently, and we all joined him. He picked up the pot and began applying stripes of red and black to their foreheads. He prayed, and Father Autry joined him, reading a prayer in Latin.

Meanwhile, off in the forest by his shrine, my father and Baghu sacrificed chickens to Ban Devi and asked for her protection of our calves and for the health of Punti Kali.

When they returned, Dilly said to me, "Nandu, these elephants will surely live a long life with all the gods they have watching over them—at least three by my count. Now if you will just say a few Tibetan Buddhist prayers, we can make it complete!" He punched me in the arm, and I punched him back.

Dilly liked to tease me about my mysterious heritage. When *Subba-sahib* found me in the jungle, I was wearing a thin red thread around my neck, a necklace worn by those of the Buddhist faith. I still do not know the fate of my birth parents, or how I came to be wandering alone in the jungle. The story I was told was that when I was two years old, I was under the protection of a pack of *dhole*, the wild dogs of the Borderlands. I survived until found by my father and Devi Kali.

For the next few hours we feasted on chicken curry, roasted goat curry, and duck curry, poured over mountains of rice. Father Autry opened a special bottle of French brandy in honor of our elephants and offered some to my father and a few of the other drivers who were brave enough to try it.

"May I propose a toast to the little jumbos? And to their devoted minder, Rita." Father Autry lifted his glass, as did the others. I had never seen Rita so happy, her face glowing and her white teeth flashing an enormous smile.

Later my father took me, Dilly, the warden, and Father Autry aside to tell us what the conservator-*sahib* had told him in private. "Nandu, Kalomutu has been sentenced to life in prison. I believe that is the end of the Maroons. The poachers who came after Pradhan are a different group, the conservator-*sahib* said. We will find them and bring them to the same justice that we brought to Kalomutu."

"The villagers are watching for the men in blue canvas sneakers," Mr. Dhungel added. "They are from across the border and will be easily spotted if they return. Ganesh Lal is our contact with the anti-poaching network we have set up." Ganesh Lal, who stood several feet behind the warden, gave me another half smile.

My thoughts went back to the man and the boy by the river and how they eyed Hira Prashad. I thought they were in awe of him, but maybe they wanted to kill him. I knew something was wrong when I saw their shoes, but even my father, a shaman, had not sensed their darkness. We were naïve, but we would not make the same mistake again.

ELEVEN

The rains failed to arrive. The monsoon season normally begins in mid-June and lasts until the first of September. We walk through mud for three months and swim through clouds of mosquitoes. But this year, June was too dry for the biting bugs. The leeches that would cling to wet leaves and drop on us had vanished. I had never lived through a year without a monsoon. The earth began to crack and the forest wilted under the hot sun. Every creature was waiting for rain. Some of the more superstitious drivers blamed the earthquake. Phirta, the most superstitious of all, said it was the start of the end of the world.

Subba-sahib was still concerned about the fate of the fifty rhinos living in the Borderlands, not just because of the poaching of Pradhan but how the rhino calves born this year would cope with the drought. Before Father Autry had left for America in mid-June, I had shared with him and *Subba-sahib* an

89

ERIC DINERSTEIN

idea—how we could use the drought and the need for rhinos to be immersed in their wallows in the forest as an easy way to keep track of them.

I repeated to *Subba-sahib* what I had learned. "Father Autry said that in the monsoon season, when the days are so hot and humid, the rhinos must avoid heat stress or they will die. Their large bodies warm up so quickly, but they cannot shed enough heat through sweating or panting or going under the shade of a tree when the air is so humid and hot. They must seek water to cool off."

"Father-*sahib* has taught you a great deal," he replied.

"Yes, but here is my idea. Father-*sahib* taught me that our rhinos can wallow up to eight hours a day in the monsoon. They are like hippos."

"Like hippos." *Subba-sahib* laughed.

"But you see, *Subba-sahib*, if they stay in their wallows for long periods, we can map the wallows and then visit each one, covering the whole area in the course of a day, and count the rhinos."

"This is a brilliant idea, Nandu. You will not only replace me as *Subba-sahib* one day, you will replace this chief wildlife warden, too!"

I turned even redder than I normally am.

"Now go and get Dilly and Indra and two elephants and prepare for this counting expedition. We shall tell the warden what we are up to."

90

Subba-sahib sent word over to the warden's office, and an hour later, Ganesh Lal sauntered into camp. He handed my father a note from the warden.

"Nandu, Ganesh Lal will accompany you on this two-day trek. One day up to Chisapani and one day back. You will cover more than forty miles. Get your supplies ready and take your rest. Now let us say good-bye to Father-*sahib*, as he leaves early tomorrow to visit his family in America."

I walked Father Autry to his bungalow, where we parted, to be reunited in seven weeks when he returned to the Borderlands.

Before dawn the next morning we were off. Indra and I rode on Hira Prashad and Dilly drove Man Kali with Ganesh Lal aboard. There were about thirty wallows we knew of in the forest between Thakurdwara and Chisapani. But most of these were around the midpoint close to the Great Sand Bar River near Lalmati.

We had passed four wallows before ten in the morning, but they were empty of rhinos and empty of water. The bottom of cracked mud was plainly visible. I was discouraged but I said to Ganesh Lal, "The next wallow coming up is the most frequently used one. Last year at this time I saw ten rhinos sharing it and sitting up to their nostrils. Only their horns and ears stuck out."

We cautiously approached the wallow, but we might as well have charged on through. It was empty. And there was no sign of any of their funny-looking three-toed tracks leading to and from it on their trails. I looked over at Ganesh but he said nothing. I wrote some lines in my field notebook and we moved on.

I could have left my notebook back at camp. We visited all thirty wallows that we knew of and found the same result. The rhinos were gone. I was so anxious, I did not know what to do once we reached the guard post at Chisapani. Part of me wanted to return as soon as we arrived and share the news with *Subba-sahib*. But it was too far and the elephants were exhausted.

The two guards posted there thought we should search the floodplain of the Great Sand Bar River. Yesterday on patrol they had seen three rhinos wallowing in one of the eddies. At dinner, two topics dominated the conversation: the drought and the rhinos. One of the guards said that cattle herders were bringing their livestock into the park because there was no fodder outside in the fields. And here at least there was water in the river. "The rest of the Borderlands is drying up," he said over a dinner of rice and fish curry.

Ganesh Lal spoke for the first time. He had a deep voice. "The rhinos must be by the river. They have to drink twice a day. I am sure that is where we will find them tomorrow. Let us take our rest now."

Ganesh Lal was right. Two miles down the floodplain from Chisapani we scared three female rhinos with young calves out of a wallow made by a small oxbow in the river where there was no current. They rumbled along the edge of the elephant grasses like tanks, huffing with each step they took. "Go back to your bathtub and cool off," I shouted to them. Indra and Dilly laughed, but Ganesh Lal barely smiled.

Our luck had changed. The wallows in the forest may have held no water, but the pools along the river were full of rhinos. My heart swelled with happiness to see them and so many with young calves. By the time we passed the cliffs below Lalmati where the banks had caved in during the earthquake, we had counted thirty rhinos. Over the next two hours along the floodplain we found ten more.

"Last year the previous game warden counted fifty rhinos," I said.

"But we took a different route. And maybe there are many more hiding in the tall grass," said Dilly, who was with me last year. Even though it was a drought, the elephant grass had very deep roots. They managed to pull the water from way down in the soil and so had already reached ten feet tall. It was impossible to find the rhinos in such high grass.

We reported our findings back to *Subba-sahib* and the warden and they seemed reassured. Perhaps the poaching of Pradhan was just an isolated incident. The rhinos were still here in numbers, but so was the drought.

July had come and gone with only a few clouds and a sprinkle or two. Two weeks more and not a drop fell. The local Tharu farmers began offering sacrifices of chickens and goats. Some approached my father, the shaman, pleading for him to reason with Ban Devi to release the rain over the Borderlands.

But it was not raining anywhere, not in northern India or in Nepal.

The rice crop was ruined.

Ganesh Lal went out again in July, this time with one of the new drivers on Jun Kali. I was to accompany him, but Rita needed help with the little jumbos so I stayed back. It had rained for two days, not in the Borderlands, but high in the mountains. Ganesh Lal reported that the river level rose quickly and it was too high to take the same route we had traversed in mid-June. He could not get to all the places where we found the rhinos before. So he stayed high on the bank and this time only counted twenty-five. We would search again for our rhinos in August.

TWELVE

The tall Tharu mailman carrying the spear waved to me. I waved to him from the back of Hira Prashad.

"Young driver, I have a letter for you."

I was amazed. I had never received a letter before. It was addressed to *Nanda Singh, the Royal Elephant Breeding Center, Thakurdwara, Nepal.* The sender was Father Autry.

July 4th, Little Rock, Arkansas

Dear Nandu, I will be heading back to Nepal at the end of July. By the time you receive this letter, I imagine, I may already be back in Thakurdwara. I am excited to be coming home. I hope the monsoon has started by now and all is well at the center.

Your trusted friend,
Father Robert Autry

When Father Autry returned from America on the first of August, my father said to him, "Father-*sahib*, you must have taken the wet winds home with you."

"*Subba-sahib*, you may be right. It poured cats and dogs every day back in Arkansas. We had flooding. I wish I could have sent some of it your way."

It soon seemed he had brought the rains back with him. On the second day of his return, I visited my tutor at his bungalow. The sky was dark and threatening rain. We sat on his veranda, watching great thunderheads stack like bulging gray balloons ready to burst. Jagged fingers of lightning spread across the sky. A howling wind bent the tree branches and blew dust into our eyes. Minutes later, at last, sheets of rain began to fall.

"Nandu, the drought is over."

"You are a shaman and a Jesuit, Father-*sahib*," I said.

"That is a useful combination, Nandu." We laughed in relief.

The rains poured down for two weeks, bringing the jungle back to life. Our new mother elephants stuffed themselves full of green grass, which made our little jumbos grow even faster. Our favorite pastime became watching the jumbos frolic in the mud wallow with the Ancient Babies.

Then, just as suddenly as they started, the rains stopped. The wind shifted to the east, and the shortest monsoon in memory was over. At least the jungle was green again. The sun came out, the temperature dropped, and every creature emerged to dry out in the gentle warmth of the early September sun—every creature, that is, except the Baba's tiger.

The next time we visited the Baba, Father Autry and I could sense that he had news, but he waited until we were done exchanging greetings and Father Autry had shared his news from America. I could see from the way his hands shook as he picked up the slate to write that he was very upset. He wrote the word *Baagh* in Devanagari.

"What is it about your tiger, Baba?" I asked.

The Baba shook his head, put his hand over his eyes, and held up two fingers.

"He's been gone for two weeks?" Father Autry asked, immediately interpreting the Baba's gestures.

I was impressed. Holy men really must understand each other.

"Perhaps the male is off looking for a mate. *Cherchez la femme*, as the French say," Father Autry continued, cocking his head and raising his thick white eyebrows.

"Baba, I read in *National Geographic* that male tigers have territories of twenty to two hundred square kilometers. He is probably out patrolling his borders," I said, proud to have remembered this fact.

I could tell the Baba appreciated our concern and effort to explain where the tiger might be. He touched the base of his throat, which to me, said that he was worried. I know that when I am worried, my throat seems to tighten.

I was almost afraid to ask. "Baba, have you found any more snares about your temple?"

He pretended to be staring about left and right and then shook his hand as if to say no. At least those poachers were no longer here.

"I will go look for any signs of him in the area beyond your temple, Baba," I offered. The Baba nodded enthusiastically.

I mounted Hira Prashad and told him we were looking for signs of the tiger. Hira Prashad is an excellent tracker, too, and when he smells a tiger, he alerts me by slapping his trunk against the ground and rumbling in a certain way.

We made wide circles, moving through the forest methodically, as my father had taught me, but we found nothing. I wished we could ask the birds, which flitted about, or the shrieking peacocks if they had seen the tiger. He was probably having a nap in the green grass somewhere, or curling the tip of his tail while he waited for prey.

I returned to pick up Father Autry and to say our good-byes to the Baba.

"I am sure your tiger will return soon," I said to the Baba. "It is his sanctuary, too!"

The Baba touched the center of his chest with two fingers, which he does when he has received both the words and the spirit of my message. It always makes me feel special when he does this.

———

The smell of brewing tea wafted across from the cookhouse. I headed over to join Rita for a mid-morning cup and to bring a pot to my father. I loved these lazy mornings in the beginning of September when the monsoon had ended. But our relaxing tea break was interrupted when Dilly came wheeling into camp on his bicycle. He had gone to Thakurdwara for supplies, but was empty-handed. He jumped from his bike before it had even stopped, his bare feet thumping on the grass.

"Nandu, get the *Subba-sahib*! A herder was attacked last night and a cow has been killed. They found a trail of blood leading into the Khata jungle. The villagers are sure it was a tiger. They are on their way to set fire to it and burn the tiger alive!"

A small, wiry man with his head down came heaving up the trail. I did not recognize him at first: I had never seen the Baba run before. He began waving his arms frantically when he saw me. I quickly understood that he thought that the villagers were after *his* tiger.

I told my father what I interpreted from the Baba's urgent arm waving.

"Dear Baba," my father said. "Tiger attacks on humans are

rare in the Borderlands. Often it is a tiger that can no longer hunt. Either it is wounded, or stuck full of porcupine quills, or a surprised tigress with cubs. Are you certain it is your tiger they are after?"

The Baba nodded his head and waved his arms. He looked at me pleadingly.

"Where are you going, Nandu?" my father asked.

"To saddle Hira Prashad. I am sure the Baba speaks the truth. We must save his tiger from being burned alive."

"Let us all go. Bring the darting kit, too."

Soon Hira Prashad was at the loading platform, so the Baba could easily climb on, and we were ready to head out.

Father Autry's car rolled into camp piloted by Dhan Bahadur. Word had traveled fast about the tiger attack. Father Autry jumped from the Land Rover and hurried to my father.

"*Subba-sahib*, there is no time to lose. We must save this animal," he said. He bowed to the Baba, and the Baba blessed him from atop Hira Prashad.

In twenty minutes, our elephants stood in a broad circle around a dense area of scrub. A ring of nearly two hundred village men surrounded us, armed with whatever they could carry. There were no Tharu men among them. These men had settled here from the hills, years ago.

"They know little about tigers and they have one purpose— to kill the tiger. If the elephants fail to drive the tiger out of the scrub, the villagers will set fire to it. Either way, they will get the Baba's tiger."

My father reached for the tranquilizer gun. He maneuvered his elephant so that Ramji could step onto a tree branch and move into position to dart the tiger. Then my father headed off to silently direct the movements of the other elephants to where we thought the tiger was hiding. I was on Hira Prashad; Dilly was on Man Kali; and my father was on Bhim Prashad. It was good to have tuskers and a brave female in the lead.

A tiger's growl stopped the five elephants behind us in their tracks. They were afraid that the tiger would jump them. *"Agat! Agat!"* I commanded Hira Prashad, pushing my fearless tusker into the dense thornbushes.

The hidden tiger roared at our approach. The young elephants started to panic. They trumpeted, and a few turned around and ran. The villagers were also fleeing. The Baba, Father Autry, and Dhan Bahadur all scrambled to the roof of the Land Rover, leaving just one person sitting inside the car: Rita.

We kept pushing our elephants through the dense thorny scrub. A tiger could easily hide in here. All of a sudden, Hira Prashad lowered his head, his tusks almost touching a male tiger crouched on the ground. I had not even seen it. The tiger rose to his feet and limped toward the tree, where Ramji was perched.

I was close enough to the tiger to see the black-and-white porcupine quills stuck in his face. At my urging, slowly, carefully, Hira Prashad kept driving the tiger closer and closer to the clearing near the base of the tree. The wounded cat roared at us, but Hira Prashad did not flinch. He kept driving it forward.

The tiger was now in range. Ramji fired the dart.

It hit the tiger in the flank. He curled back toward the dart and snarled in anger. But he was in too much pain to move. He just stood there and growled. When the villagers saw the darting happen, they stayed back to wait for a sign. Ten minutes later, the drug had done its work and the tiger's rear end started to sink to the ground. I directed Hira Prashad to the tree to fetch Ramji from his perch.

The tiger has dropped, I signaled to my father, who was still behind in the thornbushes. He rode Bhim Prashad to the tiger and joined Ramji next to him.

The villagers started running toward us led by three men in front. They would not give way. My father stayed put as they crowded around. "Move aside," the local headman snarled. "This tiger attacked a herder. He must be killed now."

"If you want to kill today, kill me!" A raspy, straining voice took our attention. It was the Baba walking through the crowd of villagers. It seemed he had floated over from the Land Rover. Because he had not spoken for so long, his voice was difficult to hear. "If you want revenge for the attack on this poor herder and the death of a cow, kill me instead, but spare this creature. He is the creation of God, and no man will touch him."

"Stand back, Baba, or you will get hurt," the second man warned. That was enough for me. I jumped off Hira Prashad and stood in front of the Baba.

The Baba knelt down and draped his arms around the sleeping tiger. "He is protected by the Baba, and he will not be harmed," I yelled. "He has been injured by a porcupine, look at his paws and his face. He cannot hunt. I know this tiger. He will not harm anyone again if we tend to his wounds."

The men ignored me and my pleas and moved in closer. The third hill tribesman in the lead group approached with his spear, ready to thrust it into the tiger. I stood in front of him and his hand came down and slapped me across my face.

It was all a blur what happened next. My tusker rushed forward and charged the man who had raised his spear and hit me. Hira Prashad trumpeted so loudly the villager dropped it and the men scattered in all directions. "*Raa!*" I shouted, and Hira Prashad stopped chasing them. The villagers were lucky my elephant listened to me.

Meanwhile, Dilly had grabbed the pliers from the darting kit and begun to pull porcupine quills from the tiger's paws. Some had lodged in and broken off. Skillfully, Dilly grabbed the end of each quill and pulled them out cleanly. Soon the tiger's paws were free of quills. But there were still the ones embedded in his muzzle. If the tiger had been gone for two weeks from the Baba's refuge, it was probably because of the quills and his pain. Two weeks would make any animal feel like it was starving, especially a tiger. I wished I could explain this to these angry men who stood glowering fifty feet away, watching our every move. But I knew they would not listen to me.

"What do we do now, *Subba-sahib*?" I asked. My face still stung where the man had slapped me.

"He will be out for a good three hours with the dose I gave him. We could bring him to camp and put him in the crate we have made to catch leopards. Then we could send him to the Kathmandu Zoo."

"He will not reach Kathmandu with these angry villagers all around us," Dilly said.

"Then let us treat him and release him back into the jungle." I spoke loudly, because I was sure no one would listen to me, the youngest person in the group.

"I agree with your idea, Nandu," said *Subba-sahib*. "We can put him in Father-*sahib*'s Land Rover and drive him across the river. We can remove the rest of the quills when we get there."

We all nodded.

"But let us stop at the stable first. I have some powders and salves. We must treat all his wounds," said my father.

My father put his head to the tiger's chest. Father Autry did the same. "I can hear the beating of his heart. It is very strong." I put my hand on the tiger's chest, too. I felt the power from touching so magical a creature run through me. Rita was suddenly there, too, stroking the tiger's soft fur. The Baba smiled and made a gesture for us to make haste. If we were to save his tiger, we had to move quickly, away from the angry mob.

The vehicle carrying the Baba's tiger reached the Belgadi River. The water level was low, so the Land Rover crossed easily.

I pushed Hira Prashad along as fast as he could go. We would reach the site in about ten minutes. All the while I talked to him.

"Hira Prashad, thank you for coming to my rescue once again. You are my brother. I can always count on you." My elephant rumbled back and lifted his trunk to touch my hand with the tip.

"I wish I had a *kuchi* to give you now, but I will make five extra for you when we return to camp."

I saw the parked Land Rover up ahead, and Hira Prashad, without any urging from me, broke into a run.

"Nandu, your tusker can practically fly. How did you make it here so quickly?" Father Autry asked. "And how on earth did Hira Prashad decide on his own to charge that man with the spear without a command?"

"Father-*sahib*, I do not know, truly. Maybe he was reading my mind. Maybe he saw him strike me and threaten the Baba."

Five of us lifted the tiger out of the vehicle and laid it on the riverbank. Indra was the strongest boy in the Borderlands. Without him, I do not think we could have lifted the heavy male. Indra headed to the riverbank and returned carrying two buckets of water. While Dilly continued removing quills from the tiger's muzzle, Rita filled cup after cup and poured the cool river water on the tiger's body. The sun was climbing and we had to prevent the tiger from overheating.

Once the quills were out, my father spread a yellow powder in the tiger's wounds. To do the same inside the tiger's cheeks, *Subba-sahib* told us to hold up the tiger's head and open its jaws again. Dilly and I grabbed from each side and Indra lifted from below. Even then, it took all three of us to hold its massive head steady.

"He must weigh over five hundred pounds," said Father Autry.

"Maybe closer to six hundred," my father said.

"Baba, you did something only a holy man can do, to protect this tiger from the mob. We are grateful to you. We will release your tiger here. Let us hope he recovers and stays away from people," said my father.

"Let us hope he also learns to stay away from porcupines. Stick with deer and the wild pig, my friend. They are much tastier," said Father Autry.

We all laughed, except for the Baba. He had stepped back behind his wall of silence.

The tiger was now beginning to stir. Quickly, our team moved back behind Hira Prashad. The tiger tried twice to stand up but staggered and sank back to the ground. Twenty minutes later, though, he was on his feet, walking off into the grassland and stiffly waving his tail.

THIRTEEN

The routine of an elephant driver—cutting grass, grazing
your animal, bathing your jumbo in the stream—has a
rhythm that soothes my mind. And nothing calms me more
than to ride alone in the jungle with Hira Prashad. We headed
deep into the forest so I could think and calm my nerves.

I had not slept well, fearing that the villagers would come
for us with their spears and shovels. If only they knew that
the escaped Maroons were the real enemy. When I thought of
those bandits, especially the one whose eye I had destroyed with
my slingshot, my chest tightened, and it was hard to breathe.
Could the poacher who killed Pradhan be one of the escaped
Maroons? Could those hill tribesmen who wanted to burn the
Baba's tiger be working for them? Then there was the Birdman
and that other fellow who tried to sell us the elephant ivory.
Could they be in the poaching ring, too, and helping the gang
to smuggle out the horns and tusks?

Maybe far from our stable across the most remote parts of the Borderlands, poaching had been going on during the summer. When the rains finally started, Ganesh Lal had taken another tour of the reserve. He did not see many of the rhinos that live between our camp and the gorge. Where had they gone?

Hira Prashad and I rode to visit our favorite view, the ridge that overlooks the sea of elephant grass bordering the Great Sand Bar River. It was now mid-September, when the Himalayan breezes blow south from Tibet, the tall grass catches the air and rolls like endless waves over the vast floodplain. The earthquake had changed the view a little. Hira Prashad and I now stood farther back, but that was the only evidence of the event. The jagged edge where the rock gave way had begun to grow over with vegetation, and the wall creepers and bee-eaters were flitting in and out of the new nest holes they had made in the clay walls. Nature's way was to keep flowing, to keep growing. I would have to do the same, but it was harder for me to do when it was humans who had disturbed the natural flow. Pradhan should not be dead. But then again, should the tiger have attacked a man and killed a village cow? Must there always be a boundary between what is wild and what is human?

I scanned the grasslands, looking out for the old elephant again, but all I saw were billowing waves of tall grass. The cotton tops swayed and undulated. I fell into a trance watching it.

"Don't you wish you could see that old mother elephant

and her calf again, Hira Prashad?" I asked. "I think if we saw that calf again, I would be able to tell if she was Devi Kali in her next life."

Hira Prashad rumbled softly back to me, as if to say *our mother.*

"Forgive me, if that is not what you said. I understand just a little of everything you say."

When I talk to Hira Prashad, I feel he is the only one who truly knows me. And even if I do not understand his rumbling fully, I feel it through my bones and muscles, right into my heart. We speak our own language.

I felt calm again and we headed home, which meant we still had two hours of quiet time together. We went to the river, then onto the path that wound its way through the dense flood-plain. Out of the corner of my eye, I saw a pack of *dhole*—the wild dogs of the Borderlands. I had not seen them in months. Their coats glowed red against the emerald-green grass. I recognized the leader with his black tail and waved to him. The others dashed for cover, but he stayed standing where two trails crossed. He scratched his paw in the sand, as if to mark the spot, and then trotted off.

I pressed my left foot gently against the back of Hira Prashad's ear so that we could go to the spot. I hopped down to get a close look at the signal my old friend had given me. The path back to the stable was clean, aside from our prints. But on the path that crossed it were the footprints of a giant elephant, larger than the ones left by Hira Prashad. The track was fresh. Hira Prashad rumbled loudly.

"I know, I know, an elephant has been here," I said to Hira Prashad. "But the footprint is far too large to be one of ours."

I grabbed a long blade of *kush* grass and curled it around the edge of the mystery elephant's front footprint, then tied it off to make a circle. I carefully folded it in my satchel to show my father when I returned to the stable.

We followed the trail of the wild elephant for a few hundred feet to where it dropped into a ravine. The banks of the gully exposed a natural salt lick. All around were the tracks of spotted deer and rhesus monkeys coming to chew on the salt deposit. In one spot, it looked like the giant elephant had pushed his tusks right into the bare walls of the mineral lick to reveal more salt. The holes he left were impressive. I could not wait to get back to tell my father that this time the village gossip was true.

There was a tusker in our jungle, and he was even larger than Hira Prashad.

PART III

THE JUMLIS

FOURTEEN

Even before the black drongos roosting in the silk cotton tree began to chirp, the pots inside the cookhouse started to clang. I stumbled over to talk to Rita, who was arranging and rearranging pots of milk on the stove to feed her charges. The chill in my bones from rising so early never seemed to leave me all day.

"Rita, you will wake the stable and Ban Devi with the noise you are making. Let the elephants rest for another hour. Even the peacocks and the red jungle fowl are only half-awake."

She ignored my joke. We had both been busy from sunup to sundown since the elephants arrived from Kanchanpur almost four months ago. Then we had been shaken by nearly losing the Baba's tiger. We barely had a chance to talk about the little jumbos. I watched her stirring and warming the milk, testing it with her finger and talking to herself.

She looked over at me. "I have no time for you now, Nandu.

The little jumbos need their vitamins, and I have hungry animals to feed. The lazy drivers from Kanchanpur do not help me at all. They sit and play cards all day. If I do not get an early start..."

"Then let me help you," I said. I grabbed a bottle.

"No, you will be in the way. I have my system."

"Forgive me, *Subba-sahib*," I said, joking.

She started to laugh. "Okay, you can help. Hold these nursing bottles while I pour in the milk. Be careful you do not make me spill any."

"*Me* make *you* spill it? That is a good one. Since you are pouring, I think you are the one to keep from spilling it."

We were both quiet, watching the warm, frothy formula fill each bottle.

"I know that I get cranky at times, Nandu. It is just... I feel that if these calves do not grow well, I will have failed in my duty."

"They are the picture of health," I said. "You could not be a better mother to them if you weighed three tons and walked around on all fours!" This made Rita's dark eyes flash at me in good humor, but she did not laugh. There was no way she was going to spill a drop.

The sun had pushed its way above the mist. October was right around the corner, when the heavy morning fog would start. I liked the fog, even if it did make it harder to see the path as we rode the elephants out for their morning feeding. Riding

116

high on Hira Prashad through the thick clouds of mist was like sailing a great boat out to sea.

Rita suddenly yodeled, triggering a stampede of tiny hooves. The two young rhinos that slept in a shed behind the cookhouse came galloping in, followed by the little jumbos, who did everything the rhinos did. Even though they got enough milk from their mothers, they still hoped for a hand-out with the other babies, which Rita usually supplied with a banana or a small *kuchi*. Nani was already there by Rita's side, waiting for her bottle, hopping up and down.

"Here, Nandu, you take the bottle for Nani. I will feed Ritu and Rona. The little jumbos will have to show their manners and wait for the rhinos to finish."

"Let me help you two," my father said, limping over from the gazebo, where he took his morning tea. His gout was acting up with the start of the morning fog season. He grabbed a bottle and made a bleating sound like a mother rhino. The two baby rhinos came trotting over to him.

"Ritu, you go to Rita. Rona, stay with me," my father said, just as if he were talking to anyone else on his staff. The rhinos obeyed, just like we do.

Rita and I looked at each other and stifled our giggles. But I could see how worn-out she was. My father noticed it, too, I am sure. He does not miss anything at our stable.

"*Subba-sahib*, the little jumbos and the Ancient Babies are already so strong," I said.

117

"These are beautiful elephants and such healthy rhinos. You are performing a valuable job, Rita," my father said. "But where are those lazy drivers to help you?"

Rita nodded over to the barracks, where the drivers were no doubt curled up on their cots, still under their quilts.

"I will find you more help, but until then Nandu will assist you. Nandu, let Indra take Hira Prashad to graze in the morning. You are assigned to help Rita mind the little jumbos while the rhinos get their morning milk. It is too much for her to manage each day."

"Yes, *Subba-sahib*. I am happy to help. Will you come with me now, before Hira Prashad takes off with Indra? I have something to show you."

"Is he developing a saddle sore, Nandu?"

"No, it is something I saw yesterday. Come see."

We walked slowly over to Hira Prashad. Indra had already climbed up on his back, ready to take him out to graze. "Indra, have Hira Prashad step into the fine dust over here," I said. Hira Prashad walked over to where I pointed, his massive tusks glistening with dew in the morning light.

The piece of kush grass that I had used to measure the footprint of the wild elephant was still folded up in my shirt pocket. With my father watching closely, I spread it on the ground, making a circle next to the footprint of my tusker.

"What is this, Nandu?"

"When I was coming back from the river with Hira Prashad, we came to the crossroads in the grassland, just up from the trail to the Great Sand Bar River. This is the footprint I found. It could be the giant male we have heard rumors about. After I measured it, we followed the tracks to the mineral lick. The male had shoved his tusks deep into the soft bank to reach the salt. The holes he left are wider than what Hira Prashad could make."

"Nandu, run and get my measuring tape."

I brought the tape back, and we laid it carefully around the edge of Hira Prashad's footprint. "Sixty-three inches," I read.

"Now, Nandu, you can do this in your head. Multiply that times two and we will know the height of Hira Prashad at the shoulder."

"Ten feet six inches, *Subba-sahib*."

We set the measuring tape around the edge of the mystery elephant's footprint. "Sixty-six inches," I said. My Father let out a low whistle. "*Subba-sahib*, he is a giant, eleven feet at the shoulder."

"Nandu, this is the biggest tusker I have seen in my life, or have yet to see. Let us hope he was just passing through the Borderlands. He must stay clear of our breeding center. Males will fight among themselves over who has the right to tend the females. This is serious."

My father looked up at Indra atop Hira Prashad, but he did

not speak right away. I could tell he was thinking through his plan. Finally, he said, "Indra, wait here for Nandu. He will join you in a few minutes." Indra nodded. Hira Prashad raised his trunk and snorted his approval, too.

My father and I walked back quickly to his bungalow, as quickly as my father can move. He pointed to the gun rack above his desk, and I climbed up on his chair to remove a rifle. Weakened by his gout, my father cannot risk climbing on a chair and falling off. I handed him his hunting rifle. He wanted it nearby in case the wild elephant entered our camp.

"But we cannot kill the giant tusker." The words flew out of my mouth before I could think better of it.

"And put our elephants, their young, and everyone in our stable in grave danger? I think not," my father said sternly.

"But they shot Pradhan," I said, quietly, trying to explain myself.

"We have a responsibility to our elephants first. It has been decided long ago."

"Of course, *Subba-sahib*," I whispered. "I know this." I imagined the wild tusker entering our camp, and our elephants chained to their posts, unable to fight. These chains—our chains—were wrong. They were against nature. I saw it clearly now.

"We will take no chances, Nandu. Be watchful when you are out grazing our tusker. Do not go alone anymore. I will tell the other drivers. You must always go in pairs on two elephants.

You and Indra will graze Hira Prashad with Dilly and his *mahout* on Man Kali. Go find Dilly now and tell him."

"But what about Rita and the morning feeding?"

"I will help her."

"But, *Subba-sahib*, it is not . . ." I trailed off. I did not know how to say that such work was beneath him, but it was.

"We must all work together to make our elephant breeding center a success and prove to the king and the conservator-*sahib* that we can do it without additional funding. This means there is no job beneath anyone, including me."

"Yes, *Subba-sahib*," I said, clearing my throat.

I only wished I could be there to see the look on Rita's face when she saw my father hobble into the cookhouse as her assistant.

———

When we had finished grazing Hira Prashad that morning, I joined the other drivers, who were sitting around the campfire, sipping tea and waiting for the midday news program. Ramji held his shortwave radio in front of his face, not to miss a word. He was the only driver in camp who owned a radio. The crackles and scratching sounds at last gave way to the calm voice of the news announcer from Radio Nepal, the one station we could receive clearly out here.

The news announcer began:

*"The lack of rain this monsoon has caused much hardship
across the kingdom. Mountain communities are facing critical
shortages of rice. His Majesty's government asks those who
have grown enough grain to donate or sell any remainder at
a discount to relief groups based in Nepalganj. His Majesty
King Birendra himself has piloted his helicopter to Jumla to
deliver sacks of rice to those in need. The villagers rejoiced upon
his arrival and praised His Majesty for coming to their aid."*

My father had his leg up on a chair. It looked so swollen. I
would brew him some tea from the *gurji* leaves to treat it.

"The announcer does not tell us the whole story," my
father said. "With the poor monsoon in the western hills, there
will be famine this year."

"You do not need to be an announcer to know this, *Subba-
sahib*," Ramji said. "You only need to look at the trail running
from the hills to the Borderlands, which is clear from the far
side of Thakurdwara. The Jumlis are coming down from the
mountains in a steady caravan. That is a sign. They may already
be starving in Jumla."

"Watermelon Belly will wish that he was still in the
Borderlands, eating his rice *palau* with raisins and almonds instead
of cornmeal mush with the Jumlis," I said. The former forest
conservator-*sahib* had tried to shut down our elephant stable.

If he had had his way, there would have been no breeding center. All of our elephants would have been marched to Chitwan under his orders. The only sign of our once-proud stable in the Borderlands would be my father and me sitting by this fire.

"We must not wish starvation on anyone," my father reminded me. "Not even our former conservator-*sahib*. He has no doubt earned his karma for his ill ways."

Ramji continued. Once he got going on a topic, he liked to hold court. "It is usually not until November that the Jumlis come down to cross to India for work as day-laborers throughout the winter. But their wheat and barley did not grow this summer," Ramji said, shaking his head like they were to be pitied.

I imagined Watermelon Belly's big stomach shrinking to normal size. Despite my father's criticism, I felt no remorse.

Suddenly, I wanted a break from the stable. I think Dilly, who is like a brother to me, sensed this and saw his chance.

"Nandu, a new film has arrived in the cinema hall in Bichia, very popular, I hear, about a clever smuggler who evades the police. We should go," he urged.

There was a lot of singing and dancing in Hindi films—too much for me, even in crime and adventure stories. "Not today, Dilly. Thanks for asking," I said.

"Nandu, come with me," Dilly pressed. "Indra can graze both elephants on our side of the border, and we can stock up on powdered milk on our way back."

"But we cannot leave Indra alone with Hira Prashad. *Subba-sahib* has told us not to take the elephants out alone." I glanced at my father, who nodded his agreement.

Indra was not worried. "The grassland near the border is too close to the busy road that runs by the Great Sand Bar River. A wild elephant will never come so close to all the oxcarts. Go to the cinema, and you can bring back samosas for me!"

"Yes! Done," said Dilly, even though Indra was speaking to me.

I looked at my father.

"Indra might be right," my father said. "But you must promise to be vigilant until you reach the main road."

"Okay," I said, only half disappointed with this outcome. "But we must also stop for the powdered formula, and I want to also visit a friend I made last time Father-*sahib* and I were in Bichia. He is a doctor."

"Great," said Dilly. "Maybe I can ask him to look at my knee, which aches in the fog."

"You are getting gout, old man, just like *Subba-sahib*," I said. Dilly hit me in the head with a *kuchi* he pulled from his pocket.

We were halfway to Bichia when we came upon a wooden wagon stuck in a muddy rut. The driver flicked his whip at the scrawny horse tied to the wagon, who strained against his reins but was unable to move it. We jumped off our elephants to help.

"Indra, see if you can push the wagon out of the muck. Dilly and I will hack some thick branches to place under the wheels."

"Indra could lift that wagon out by himself, like the hero in the Hindi cinema," Dilly said. Indra smiled and shook his head.

We quickly returned with our arms loaded with branches. The wagon was still stuck in the rut. Indra walked toward us with his head down.

"He is not friendly. He got angry with me when I offered to push from behind while the horse pulled. He called me a rat-eating Tharu and told me to get lost, or he would whip me, too."

We watched the man get down and struggle to push the wagon. He shouted curses at the horse. I hated to see him abuse his horse for his own stupidity.

I called to the stubborn man, "Here, put these branches under the wheels, and we will rope our elephants to the front of the wagon and have them pull you out. It is too much strain on your horse."

Dilly called for Man Kali, and Indra steered Hira Prashad to move to the front of the wagon. Indra was still angry with the man. He kept his head down. Hira Prashad was not listening to Indra. I wondered if I should climb up and take over. Instead, Hira Prashad stepped behind the wagon. The man turned around. He was wearing a patch over his left eye and had a dark beard.

"I told you to get away from behind the wagon. Get that elephant out of here. It will scare my horse."

I recognized that voice. But from where? Something started moving under the canvas covering the wagon. Then there were three of them bumping around. Maybe he was stealing wild boar piglets from the jungle, I thought. But they would be squealing by now.

Hira Prashad grabbed the edge of the canvas with his trunk and yanked it loose. Sticking out from under the canvas were the thin legs of three girls. Their ankles were bound together. They started to shout, but their mouths were gagged and their voices muffled.

The man drew a long knife and came straight for Dilly and me.

"Watch out, Nandu!" Dilly shouted.

Hira Prashad rushed in and swung his trunk around and knocked the man to the ground. He got back on his feet quickly but dropped his knife and ran. Before I could stop him, my elephant began chasing the man down the road. The smuggler's only chance of escape was to leap into the swirling river below. We watched as he flailed in the water until he disappeared downstream.

"Nandu, I recognized that voice," said Dilly. "It was him, that Maroon last year on the Gularia Road. He was the one who told us to give up our gold and cash or be killed. I remember that voice, like spilling gravel."

Yes, of course, he was the one I hit in the eye with the rock fired from my slingshot. I took his eye out. That is why he was wearing the patch.

"Dilly, he recognized us, too."

"Yes, and thankfully, this time we had Hira Prashad."

"Come on, Nandu, we need to free the girls."

"You go. Let me look after Hira Prashad for a moment. I will join you."

Hira Prashad stood at the cliff looking downriver as if he were guarding against the Maroon's return from down below. I put my hand on the front of my tusker's quivering trunk but no sound came out, at least not one I could hear.

"How did you know this Maroon carried captives in the back of his wagon? Did you smell their fear? Did you hear them?"

Hira Prashad's mind was elsewhere. He rumbled angrily, his ears held wide and his trunk sampling the air, trying to pick up any scent of the Maroon. He swung his head back and forth in defiance. Hira Prashad could have stepped on Eye Patch and killed him, but he let him go. I wonder if he, too, had second thoughts. My tusker turned his massive head to focus on the river below. We stayed for a while until he was satisfied the Maroon was gone.

FIFTEEN

Hira Prashad and Man Kali stood on either side of the three girls like they were elephant calves, protecting them. Man Kali rumbled deeply to Hira Prashad, who answered, then raised his trunk into the air, as if checking for any further signs of trouble.

The girls' skinny wrists and ankles were red and raw from the chafing ropes.

"Where did you come from?" Dilly asked, even though it was obvious. We could see from the way they were dressed and from their jewelry that the girls were from Jumla.

None of them answered. I moved closer to offer them some food.

"Are you hungry?"

From my satchel I handed them part of our lunch, some

boiled rice and raisins I had wrapped in *sal* leaves. The girls hesitated; only the littlest one, about age ten, took the leaves and gave some to the other two.

"Where were you going?" asked Indra. No reply. The girls did not even look at him. They might never have been outside Jumla, or seen an elephant, until now.

"Please do not send us back," said the youngest, looking directly at me. She then ventured to touch Hira Prashad's trunk before I could warn her that he did not like to be approached by strangers. She patted and rubbed his skin, and my elephant graciously let her. The other girls seemed scared, but this one was fearless.

"We should not wait around here," Dilly said. "I guess we will take them back to the stable."

"Yes," I agreed. "They can wash up and eat properly, and *Subba-sahib* can give them salve for their cuts." I turned back to the girls, who were throwing the empty *sal* leaves to the side of the road. "Where did you come from today?" I tried again.

The oldest one finally spoke. She pointed north and said, "We came from Chisapani this morning. The man who led us down the mountain trail from Jumla put us in this wagon he had waiting at the bazaar. He told us to make no noise or he would toss us into the river. He was taking us to India to find work in a factory."

I did not know what to say.

Dilly focused on the practical details. "We will let the horse free. He will find his way back to Chisapani on his own. The wagon we will push into the river. Come on, Indra."

Indra put all of his anger into his task. While Dilly freed the horse, Indra arranged the elephants in front of the wagon and hauled it out of the rut. Then alone Indra pushed the wagon to the edge of the overhang. He shouted at the river below and sent the wagon flying off the cliff.

The two older girls looked scared and sad. One seemed about thirteen, my age, and the other eleven, but it was hard to tell with Jumlis. Life is harder in the mountains, and the cold dry air of their high villages makes people look much older than they are.

Dilly commanded Man Kali to kneel, and he showed them how to sit on the saddle. Indra gently lifted the little one and put her in front of him behind Hira Prashad's ears. Dilly and I walked in front the whole way to Thakurdwara.

Taking care of the girls distracted me from what we had experienced. We spoke out of earshot of them.

"Dilly, the Maroons escaped from the Birganj jail during the earthquake."

"Yes, and all five of them were recaptured the next day. What are you driving at?"

"Dilly, when the Maroons raided Mohanpur last year, and you arrived with *Subba-sahib* and Ramji in the nick of time, there were seven of them, plus Kalomutu and a younger boy with them who ran off. Kalomutu is now in prison, and the five that fled the jailbreak in Birganj are now back behind bars. That still leaves three."

"No, I would say one Maroon and a boy. I doubt we will ever see Eye Patch show his face around here again. And who knows, I'll bet he couldn't swim. Maybe he drowned on his way down the river to India."

I wished I could be as certain about life as Dilly.

Unfortunately, Dilly's day at the Hindi cinema floated downriver with the wagon, but it seemed he had already forgotten about it. Whenever there was a crisis, there was no better person to have around. Ever since Indra had been made *mahout* of Hira Prashad, I spent more time with Indra and less with Dilly. But even though Dilly was six years older than me, and Indra was closer in age, today it was like nothing had changed; Dilly and I were brothers again, reading each other's mind. Just like me and Hira Prashad.

We had a two-hour march back home. Dilly started singing an old mountain tribe song, about a herder who had lost his favorite sheep during a snowstorm but found it again, sheltered under a rock. The littlest girl knew it, too, and she started to sing along.

As we walked along the dirt road, our moods lifted and we began to kick up the brilliant red leaves of the *kamno* trees that had blown to the ground, carried by the fresh late-September breeze. So many questions swirled in my mind. Why would these girls leave their home alone? How could they have worked in a factory in India without their parents? Where were they to live?

My father was standing talking to Rita when we entered camp. "*Subba-sahib*, we have some guests who need your help. They have rope burns on their wrists and ankles. And I think they are very hungry."

The elephants dropped their knees to the ground, and Indra handed the youngest girl off to me. I held her arm, as she had trouble regaining her footing. Two hours on the elephants had made the girls' legs go numb.

Each girl gestured *namaste* to my father, and he nodded. He signaled for Indra to bring them something to sit on while he looked at their wounds. Indra came running back carrying three heavy *sal* chairs.

"Nandu, cut some fresh papaya and pick up my medicine bag. And grab some honey from the cookhouse to mix with my powders."

My father was the most skilled medicine man in the Borderlands, and I loved to watch him work. He washed the girls' wounds in warm water and dried them with clean gauze that we used for the elephants when they developed saddle sores. He mixed together the powder from the dried leaves of the *bhanti* and *pudinah* plants.

"Come, girls, this will cool the burning." I brought him the papaya and honey and he mixed it all in a bowl. Then he spread it on their rope wounds and wrapped them in gauze. Once their wounds were tended to, they sat back in their chairs and drank the lemon tea that Rita and Tulsi had brought them.

"Tulsi, Rita, stay with our guests. I want to talk for a moment with Nandu and Dilly. Indra, take Hira Prashad to graze, but stay close to the other elephants."

Indra bowed and left. Dilly and I followed my father back to the gazebo, where he liked to have important conversations. When we were all seated on the schoolhouse chairs, he said, "Tell me everything that happened."

I looked at Dilly, who nodded to me and spoke first. "*Subba-sahib*, we found them on the road in the back of a wagon headed to India. They were hungry and scared so we brought them here."

"Why were their wrists tied together?"

"The wagon driver had been paid to deliver them to India to work in a factory."

Dilly was not getting to the point, so I jumped in. "*Subba-sahib*, the driver was the Maroon. The one that I shot in the eye with my slingshot on the Gularia Road."

My father leaned forward, hands on his knees, his face creased in concern. "Go on, Nandu."

"Except now he wears an eye patch. He came at us, but Hira Prashad chased him off. He jumped over the bank and into the river. That is the last we saw of him."

"There must be more to this story. The Maroon driving

them would not bind their wrists and then run away unless there was something illegal here. In the meantime, we must figure out what to do with them. For the night, ask Tulsi to make room for them in her hut. You boys will bring the extra cots. Tomorrow, we will figure out a plan."

For the rest of the afternoon and evening, the girls from Jumla never left my side. Rita was busy with Nani, the Ancient Babies, and the little jumbos. That was fine by me, except I had to go for my weekly visit to talk to Devi Kali. I always brought Hira Prashad along, too.

"I'll be back soon," I told the girls, who had finally told us their names.

"We will come with you," the oldest girl said, no longer so scared. Her name was Kabita. I did not want all the girls to come along, but I was happy that they were starting to talk to us more.

I should be welcoming; I remembered my horrible night in the jail after I was accused of killing the other Maroon. The kindness of my friends and family was the only thoughts that comforted me. And these girls had no family to rely on. No one.

"Okay," I said. "We will walk with my elephant. He always comes with me." I did not explain why.

The five of us left, walking past the stable and out on the trail to the bridge, just past Gobrela village. On the other side of the bridge stood the giant *mohwa* tree, beneath which my

Devi Kali was buried near the banks of the Belgadi River. Across the way stood a large fig tree.

We stood by the grave in silence. I placed lemongrass on it. The youngest girl found more lemongrass near the river and started to pull some stalks. She walked back and added them to my pile.

Hira Prashad helped, too. He reached down and picked up some tussocks of lemongrass in his trunk and shook the clods of dirt clinging to the roots. He placed them at my feet and stood back. Was he saying, *She was my mother, too?* I placed Hira Prashad's gift with the rest of the lemongrass on Devi Kali's grave.

The girls stood quietly, watching, and I explained.

"Here is where my elephant is buried, the one I rode before Hira Prashad. Her name was Devi Kali. I mean, it is still Devi Kali. She was like a mother to me, except even kinder and gentler. It was she who first found me in the jungle by Clear Lake, when I was only two."

I told them my whole story. They listened in silence, except for the middle one, who had not said a word since we met. Her eyes filled with tears and she began to weep. But I had to finish my story. "If she had not heard or smelled me in the tall grass, the hyenas would have carried me off. I am so grateful to Devi Kali. I miss her every day."

"At least she loved you like a mother should love her child. Our mother is dead, too, and our stepfather sold us to that man with the eye patch for ten sacks of rice," the tearful one said.

We were quiet for a moment, then the oldest girl, Kabita, spoke. "Nandu, Jayanti is my younger sister. I am thirteen and she is twelve."

"Thirteen is my age, too," I said. "Excuse me. I did not mean to interrupt!"

Kabita smiled. Then the little one, who was called Kanchi, stepped forward. "I am ten, but I am not their sister. I am on my own. We are all from the same village in Jumla. That man with one eye spoke with our fathers."

Kabita picked up her story. "That one-eyed man driving the wagon had promised our families that he would take us to a factory in Lucknow. Then he would collect our wages and bring the cash back to Jumla, minus his fee for arranging work and transporting us to India."

"How could your fathers sell you to him?"

"There is famine in Jumla. By sending us away, there are fewer mouths to feed. Plus we would be able to bring in more money from India. That is what our stepfather said when we left."

I did not say what I knew to be true. Their stepfather had sold them permanently to the Maroon. There would be no back-and-forth with money.

Kanchi spoke again. She did not hold back. "You have met this horrible man before, Nandu. I heard you say."

"Yes, I have. I will tell you that story some other time."

I could not imagine why people abandon their children to

the world. I had long forgiven my parents. I believed that they must have had a good reason for leaving me by Clear Lake. But these men were never to be trusted. *How could they sell their own children for rice, even in a famine?*

Kanchi spoke up. "Nandu, your beautiful elephant-mother saved you. Just like Hira Prashad saved us when he ripped the canvas cover off the wagon. How did he know to do that? Did you tell him?"

I shook my head. "I think he sensed you were in danger. I cannot explain it. Elephants are wise in ways we do not understand."

I wished that I could have shared my secret with them, that Hira Prashad was the son of my mother, Devi Kali. But then I thought of the secret my father shared with me, the one nobody but Ramji knows. And then I thought of the secrets shared with me by the Baba, and Father Autry. And my own private story of killing a Maroon in self-defense. Now the girls had shared with me things not to be repeated, about being sold for sacks of rice.

The five of us, standing before Devi Kali's grave, all had something deeply in common. Hira Prashad was sold away from his mother, just as the girls had been sold by their step-father and father. I had lost my parents, and the only mother I knew, as all of us had, learning at the youngest age that the world can be a harsh place, and family can grow from things other than blood.

I knelt down and put my hand on Devi Kali's grave. *It is family just the same,* I told her. *Perhaps stronger because we have the gift of knowing great loss and receiving great love all the same.*

Kabita knew I needed a moment alone with my tusker. She linked arms with Jayanti and Kanchi and led them back toward camp. When they were out of sight, I bowed at my mother's grave. We had performed this ritual enough together that the moment Hira Prashad saw me kneel, he did the same.

SIXTEEN

The fields bordering the elephant stable had become a carpet of golden-yellow against the dark green jungle. The mustard was in its October bloom. The fields must be the same color in Jumla, too, because I awoke to hear Jayanti singing about the sun shining on the fields and the bright yellow mustard turning golden. I walked into the cookhouse to find Rita and the Jumlis tending the fire and mixing powdered milk.

They burst into a Nepali folk song about a rooster waking everyone up. Rita had already made herself a friend to these girls, who needed a friend so badly.

"Oh no, our singing has wakened the snoring Nandu," Rita said.

"I do not snore!" I said, falling for Rita's teasing.

The Jumlis, all three of them, suddenly bowed. I looked around to see that my father had entered the room. Rita quickly handed him a steaming mug of tea.

"Such lovely songs," he said. "I thought there was a shama that had flown into the cookhouse." The girls smiled. My father was referring to the most beautiful singer in the forest, the bird we call the white-rumped shama.

"Rita, it looks like you have plenty of help now with the feeding of your young animals," my father said. "I was going to step in, but now I see there is no need."

"Thank you, *Subba-sahib*, but yes, it is as if Ban Devi has given us exactly what we needed."

"We are all grateful," said my father. "Though the girls may not be able to stay. They may want to return to their families."

"No!" cried Kanchi, the youngest and boldest. "We cannot return. Our families are not there. And if they are, they would only sell us again!"

My father raised his eyebrows, then rested his hand gently on Kanchi's head. "Then you will all stay until we get more information."

Rita called out for the rhino babies to come for their milk. The Jumlis were surprised to see rhinos careen into the cookhouse begging for their bottles by extending their curved upper lips. Next the trunks of two baby elephants appeared in the doorway, followed by a third. Kabita gasped, and she slowly moved closer to touch their waving trunks. Even the older girls were growing comfortable with our animal kingdom.

Last but not least, Nani scooted through the maze of elephant legs to claim her rightful place at the head of the line.

"A fawn!" Kanchi squealed with delight.

Rita went into commander mode, handing out bottles. "Kabita, you feed Nani. Jayanti, you take Ritu. Kanchi, would you like to feed Rona? She is feisty and may try to push you around at first."

The youngest girl nodded. Rita had made a good call. Kanchi liked a challenge and would prove she was up to handling the rhino calf.

"Nandu, do not just stand there. Keep the elephants occupied until the girls can attend to them."

My father winked at me. It made him happy to see all of us, the youngest people in camp, taking so much responsibility.

After Nani and the rhinos had been fed, I showed our newcomers around the stable and the shed where the Ancient Babies slept at night. The barracks were empty, and I pointed out my room. Afterward, I led them down to the special grove where my father went to pray to Ban Devi. I did not expect to find him there today, standing in a trance-like state. Perhaps he was seeking guidance from the forest goddess who watches over us to help him decide the right thing to do about the girls. I motioned for them to be quiet, and we backtracked quietly to the stable.

I was on my way back to meet Indra to take Hira Prashad out to graze, when I heard my father call to me. I waited for him near the gazebo.

"Nandu, I have thought hard about this matter and prayed

for guidance from Ban Devi. I am afraid you will not like this, but we must inform the police about the girls from Jumla. They were sold into captivity. That is the truth, whether the parents were aware of it or not."

I shook my head. "*Subba-sahib*, please, they—"

"I am sorry, Nandu. These girls are too young to be on their own without their families."

"Father, they are no different from me, when you found me by the Clear Lake. Their mother is dead and their stepfather sold them for sacks of rice. They were supposed to go to India to work in a factory in Lucknow, until we rescued them. The Maroon smuggling them into India was threatening to kill them if they tried to escape."

"That Maroon may come back for them."

"I do not think so. The last we saw him, he had tumbled into the river, after Hira Prashad chased him over the edge of a high ridge above it."

"Good. But the police should pursue the man nonetheless."

As much as I wanted the police to investigate the Maroon, I did not trust them after my stay in the jail in Gularia. They did not listen to children.

"But the police will take the girls back to Jumla! You heard what Kanchi said. They would only be traded again for more rice!"

This made my father pause. Whenever he paused, I knew I

had a window of opportunity to persuade him of my point of view.

"What if we tell the police that they came down from Jumla with their relatives to sell their baskets full of tangerines in the bazaar? That their relatives told them to wait and, for some reason we do not know, left them behind?"

"I do not think the police would believe that, Nandu. Besides, it is a lie."

We were interrupted by three shrieking girls being chased by three baby elephants, two rhinos, and a spotted deer fawn. They stopped in the middle of the camp out of breath. The little jumbos moved in, nudging and pushing them not to stop. The girls reached out and hugged them gently.

"It looks like the calves have accepted their extra caretakers," I said.

Rita came up to them, with her mother. *"Subba-sahib,"* she said. "You can see that these girls are more caring for the little jumbos than those *mahouts* from Kanchanpur."

"And you need all the help you can get. Rita, you have done a fine job. Do you think you can teach these girls to do what you do?"

"Oh yes, *Subba-sahib!*"

"Rita, these little jumbos are far too young to learn the first thing about being a working elephant. The calves need all the attention we can give, even more than what the *mahouts* provide who are assigned to them. These calves are babies and need constant supervision so they don't get into trouble. We will put the girls on a two-week probation. If they do well, maybe they can stay, and we will pay them."

———

Later that afternoon, I headed over with Hira Prashad to the Baba's temple to drop off his monthly load of firewood by myself. No need to bring Indra for a short trip away from the grasslands where we'd seen wild elephant tracks. Along the trail, I did see the familiar footprints of the large male tiger, the one we had saved from the villagers. He was back in his territory. The Baba must be so pleased to have his neighbor return.

As we approached, the Baba was standing outside his hut. He had extrasensory powers and always knew we were coming before we appeared.

Since the release of his tiger, he had retreated back to silence, so I was surprised to hear him speak.

"Put down your load, Hira Prashad, and let Nandu share some tea with me." He walked up to my elephant and fed him the stalk of sugarcane he always brought for my tusker.

"Baba, your tiger is back. I am so pleased."

The Baba nodded, his face smiling.

The jungle was at peace again, even if we still worried about the new tusker and the return of the Maroon. But Kalomutu was in prison. The Maroons were finished. What could one Maroon do against all of us?

The Baba poured tea while I told him about our encounter with the Maroon with the one eye, the one I had struck with a rock fired from my slingshot on the Gularia Road. I told him about the girls from Jumla who thought they were headed to a factory in Lucknow.

"My dear friend, these girls were not sold to work in a factory. Do you remember that I once owned one? That was a lie that Maroon told."

I nodded. I remembered the Baba's story. And his secret I carried about children dying in a fire that took place in his factory and the responsibility he felt for their deaths.

"Nandu, they were sold to be at the service of men. That is the hard truth."

I struggled to put into words what was in my head. "Baba, when the villagers were about to kill your tiger, you said that if it happened, you would accept it as fate. You would forgive their ignorance. But I cannot forgive them."

"Why not, Nandu?" rasped the Baba.

"Those men were from the same village robbed by the Maroons. We captured the Maroons and returned to those villagers their precious jewels and cash. But that was all forgotten. They stood against us, even when we explained the

145

truth. I could never trust them. They would even turn over the Jumlis to the police if they would gain from it. I will never accept their ignorance."

"Nandu, acceptance of the world does not mean you join in their ignorance. You and Dilly and Indra and Hira Prashad saved the girls from a fate worse than drowning. That death is only once. What the girls were facing, where they were headed, is to die a little every day."

I nodded.

"My dear friend, there is evil and extreme cruelty in this world. Not everywhere, but I am afraid you know too much about it at such a young age."

I did not respond. The Baba closed his eyes and mumbled some prayers. He had the power to see things, like my father. A few minutes later he opened them again.

"Nandu, I believe this Maroon is full of vengeance, much of which is focused on you. You must watch out for his return."

SEVENTEEN

I n a previous life, the Jumli girls must have been elephants, or elephant drivers. I cannot otherwise explain how quickly they took to their new roles as assistant caretakers of the little jumbos. They sang to them and fed them their treats. They learned from the drivers how to make *kuchis*, tiny ones, just for the young calves' small mouths. After the calves rolled in the dirt, something they wanted to do as often as possible, Kanchi would slap the fine dust off them with a piece of burlap cloth. Kabita and Jayanti tossed them sticks and balls, and the baby elephants threw them back.

All three girls wore their hair in a thick dark braid that slid back and forth over the backs of their blouses. Jayanti was the quiet one, but you could tell how smart she was. She was the first to learn to read and write under Tulsi's instruction. I thought of asking her to accompany me to my lessons with

Father Autry, because I knew she would soon hold her own. She mostly cared for Shanti Kali, the jumbo who liked to try to tug on Jayanti's long braid.

"Owww, you are hurting me," Jayanti would say, pretending. Then she would laugh and kiss the little jumbo on her forehead.

Kabita was the talkative one and made me laugh with her funny comments. She even made *Subba-sahib* laugh, and that is hard to do.

"*Subba-sahib*, look at this naughty Mina Kali. She never wants to take a nap."

"How can she, Kabita, when you play with her nonstop?" He laughed.

Then there was Kanchi. If girls could be allowed to become *mahouts*, she would have excelled. She was a natural around animals and totally unafraid of the elephants. And somehow they respected the shortest person in camp. Maybe because Hira Prashad dropped his ears forward for her to grab them so he could lift her with his trunk over his head. I thought I was the only one he allowed to mount this way.

I decided that morning to allow Kanchi to accompany me and Hira Prashad to Clear Lake to show her where I was found. I was going to leave a gift for the *dhole* who protected me.

Kanchi was the first to spot the *dhole* on the trail to Clear Lake. "They are so beautiful, Nandu. We have them in Jumla, too."

We had stopped at Clear Lake for Hira Prashad to drink and for us to stretch our legs. I told Kanchi my whole story.

"You are so lucky to have been brought to the stable, Nandu. To live with all these animals is a dream come true. If you had not found us with Hira Prashad, we would be inside a factory now somewhere in India and not by this beautiful lake."

I thought of what the Baba had told me about the true fate the girls would have faced, a life far worse than a factory. But I stayed silent, reaching over to smack Kanchi on the arm. A large horsefly had landed and was about to feast. Then five more landed and another bit me on the arm.

Without speaking, we both climbed up onto Hira Prashad to get away from the swarm of flies. Hira Prashad was as happy to move away as we were.

On our way back to camp, my elephant suddenly thumped his trunk down and let out a low roar. Something had deeply upset him. A rifle shot made him start to run. I thought the poachers had returned.

"*Raa!*" I shouted, but Hira Prashad barely stopped. We were racing back to the stable. The whole time I could hear Hira Prashad emitting an angry rumble.

"What's wrong?" yelled Kanchi, clearly frightened, but hanging on to the saddle bravely.

"I don't know, but Hira Prashad knows something we don't!" I replied. "Hang on tightly!"

When we entered camp, we saw a smashed cot in a heap

149

near the cookhouse. Bundles of grass piled up for the afternoon feed lay scattered across the courtyard. My father approached holding his rifle in his one good arm. Next to him was the government vet, who had come to check on the little jumbos. He came every month now that we had so many to look after.

"Nandu, we had a visit from the giant tusker. He stormed through camp, but fortunately all the elephants and the calves were grazing by the river. He smashed the cot in anger. I think he was looking for the three calves from Kanchanpur because he stayed and turned around several times by their tethering poles."

"Was anybody hurt?"

"Fortunately, no. Ramji threw a burning log from the fire pit at him. When he would not leave, I fired a shot over his head. He ran into the forest. I tracked him for a while but he is gone."

"Is it true what they say about his size?"

"He is bigger than Hira Prashad, Nandu, and his tusks are a foot longer," my father said.

"They are the biggest I have ever seen," said the vet.

"Are Jayanti and Kabita safe?"

"Yes, they are down by the river with Rita. They are learning how to bathe the little ones. Come, let us go and watch. I do not think the male will come back through camp for a good long while."

Walking alongside us was one of the oldest drivers from Kanchanpur, who drove Punti Kali. His name was Narayan.

"Narayan, does the *Subba-sahib* of Kanchanpur or any of you drivers know which tusker bred Punti Kali or the other three females now here?" asked my father.

"No, *Subba-sahib*. When the females were ready to breed we let them out into the jungle. The palace told us to do this. If we had kept them close to the stable we might have seen the male who bred them. One of our drivers said that they saw a giant male with big tusks approach Punti Kali, but the driver was a drunk so no one believed him. *Subba-sahib*, we heard reports of this massive tusker like you did. But I did not believe there could be a tusker bigger than Hira Prashad. Now I have seen him with my own eyes."

"I believe we now know who fathered the three calves from Kanchanpur. I think he has come to check on them," my father said.

"He will challenge Hira Prashad," I said, fearful that this tusker could endanger not only my elephant but our little jumbos.

"We will protect our elephants and our calves," my father said resolutely.

But I could not shake the feeling that there was an imminent threat to our happiness, whether it was this mysterious tusker or the Maroon who would never forget me.

151

EIGHTEEN

What can be a more humble treat than a fistful of unhusked rice mixed with lumps of rock salt and dried molasses and wrapped in the coarse leaves of elephant grass? But to my Hira Prashad and the other elephants and even the little rhinos, these were the tastiest of morsels.

"Hira Prashad, do you dream about *kuchis* when you sleep?" I asked. He banged his trunk on the ground and then lifted it, exposing his wide mouth for me to stuff in another *kuchi*.

Hira Prashad stopped begging and began to rumble. He held his ears out straight. I rubbed his trunk, unsure of what he was trying to tell me. "Is this a warning, my friend?" I asked him, still waiting for the day when I would be able to communicate with him as easily as I did with Dilly or Rita.

Minutes later, I heard the sound of a car engine. It was the conservator-*sahib*, his driver, and Doctor-*sahib*, the veterinarian. This was what Hira Prashad was telling me.

"What is he up to now?" I whispered to Hira Prashad. He flapped his ear with enough force that it snapped, like a white sheet drying in the wind.

I knew the conservator-*sahib* lived in eastern Nepal. Why would he be coming so early and just before Tihar, the holiest festival of the year? I walked over to join my father, who had emerged from his gazebo to greet the visitors. As they approached, my father nodded to both men.

"Conservator-*sahib*. What brings you here so close to Tihar?"

"Duty calls, *Subba-sahib*. Mine and yours. Have you heard the latest news from Kathmandu?"

My father shook his head. We had no source for news. The batteries in Ramji's shortwave radio had died, and we had not yet made it back to the Bichia bazaar.

Mr. Rijal, the forest conservator-*sahib*, continued, "You know that Kalomutu was put away in prison forever. Now his gang of Maroons that had escaped from the Birganj jail during the earthquake were sentenced to life imprisonment, too."

Ramji, who was the most superstitious of the drivers, was sitting nearby and spat into the fire. "Kalomutu's body may be in jail but the evil spirit within him will move on to another living soul on the outside," he said. Ramji always had the darkest interpretation of things.

I was surprised that my father did not tell Mr. Rijal about the one-eyed Maroon. I wondered if his silence was to protect the three girls from being sent back to Jumla.

"Ramji, the Maroons are finished, I tell you," said the conservator-*sahib*. "I have read Mr. Dhungel's report. The warden and Ganesh Lal have concluded that the rhino poachers were either rogue poachers or part of another gang. They had nothing to do with the Maroons who are all in jail in Kathmandu. Let us focus now on the raising of these calves. I will go pick up the warden and when we finish our paperwork we will return for our monthly inspection of our new elephants."

My father could not speak. Mr. Rijal must have read *Subba-sahib*'s thoughts, or my father the shaman allowed him to do so.

"But I see, *Subba-sahib*, you are concerned still about our rhinos. I will talk to Mr. Dhungel and Ganesh Lal. We will see if we can bring more guards to the Borderlands."

My father used the moment of his departure to speak up again. "Doctor-*sahib*, you must reason with the palace and this new conservator-*sahib* who knows nothing about the Borderlands. We need more armed guards stationed not just here, but at Chisapani and the Bheri Valley. I fear the rhinos are still at risk."

"*Subba-sahib*, I share your concerns. But it will be hard to convince the palace. The northern Borderlands are now a national park. Besides, there are two guard posts, one here and one up at the gorge of the Great Sand Bar River at Chisapani.

The two ranger units can cover the fifteen miles in between. That is what Mr. Dhungel will tell his boss, the conservator."

"It may be a national park but in name only. Do you think Dhungel-*sahib* ever strays from his office? If he does, it is to walk a few steps to buy betel nut in the nearby tea stall. And this Ganesh Lal. I have seen him out in the jungle only twice, and for just a few days. How much evidence could he have gathered?"

The doctor-*sahib* smiled.

My father went on. He was growing upset, which is rare for him to express in front of others. "Those guard posts do not have enough men to protect the area. The few who are stationed there in Chisapani are drunk on *raksi* half the time. Their rifles are ancient, and they are only allotted a few bullets. There will be no protection for those rhinos if poachers return. There are fifty rhinos between here and Chisapani along the Great Sand Bar River. But this summer at our count at the wallows we could find only forty. And those rhinos that live in the Bheri Valley to the north are in grave danger."

"I will see what I can do, *Subba-sahib*. You have information we do not have in Kathmandu."

The conservator-*sahib* came back in the jeep with Mr. Dhungel and Ganesh Lal. Maybe he would listen to my father about his concern for the park's rhinos after the inspection of the elephants.

"Conservator-*sahib*, Warden-*sahib*, come look at how well the young calves are doing," said my father.

He motioned to Rita, who put two fingers in her mouth and let out a piercing whistle. The three little jumbos came rushing over, followed by the rhino calves. The warden jumped behind my father, faster than I have ever seen him move. The little jumbos were not sure about the new guests and quickly ran back to Rita, Kanchi, Jayanti, and Kabita. The girls handed out sugarcane to calm the jumbos and the Ancient Babies.

"And who are these girls, *Subba-sahib*? Where did they come from?" said the conservator-*sahib*.

"They help look after the calves. Our new drivers are too busy caring for the three mother elephants *and* Punti Kali to watch the little ones all day, too."

"Are you daft? Young girls cannot train elephant calves!"

I had not seen this insult coming. My heart began to race. But my father let the conservator's words fly over his head like a frightened bird.

Stay calm, Nandu, I could hear my father say. *Sometimes while you are worrying, things work out for themselves.*

"Elephant trainers will tell you, Conservator-*sahib*, that you do not even try to teach young elephants their commands until they reach six years of age," my father explained in a patient voice. "These elephants are not yet two. They are like infants.

What they need are staff to stay with them and keep them out of trouble, like extra minders. Is that not so, Doctor-*sahib*?"

"He is right, Conservator-*sahib*. The only thing these young elephants can do at this age is make mischief. Look how they respond to these girls!"

The little jumbos stuck out their trunks, begging for more sugarcane from their caretakers. Mr. Rijal turned his gaze back to my father. I could sense another frightened bird fluttering before the words even left his mouth.

"You are the officer in charge of His Majesty's Royal Breeding Center, *Subba-sahib*, not an orphanage."

The girls kept their heads down so no one would see the tears that I knew had sprung up in their eyes.

Yes, you fool, my father is running an orphanage.

My father sensed my anger rising and he put his hand on my shoulder and squeezed it gently. "These young girls have lost their mother and father, Conservator-*sahib*. They are staying with their aunt Tulsi, the mother of our driver Dil Bahadur and Rita over here—they are all the girls have left for family."

We get rid of Watermelon Belly, and he is reincarnated as Boney Face. What did we do to deserve such karma?

Boney Face shook his head. He turned and walked to his jeep without saying good-bye. The warden signaled to the driver that they were leaving. My anger had been replaced by astonishment. It was the first time I had heard my father tell a lie. Yet I had never felt so proud of him. I put my hand on his, which was still resting on my shoulder.

That night, there was no singing from the cookhouse. I had grown so used to the girls' voices that the camp became suddenly quiet and sad. I stopped by for a visit. When I entered, Kabita and Jayanti dropped their heads. They worked at night on a loom Tulsi had borrowed, weaving wool by kerosene lamps, which only pierced the darkness here and there. But I could still see their tear-streaked faces.

Kanchi spoke. "Please ask *Subba-sahib* not to send us away, Nandu."

"Do not worry. *Subba-sahib* knows you belong here with us. He said what he did today, about Tulsi being your aunt, to be sure that no one can take you away. I have never known him to speak anything but the truth. He must believe your fate is to live here, with us."

Kanchi smiled an enormous smile, and both Kabita and Jayanti raised their faces. Each girl beamed so brightly it felt like daylight breaking in the night. It was the smile of knowing that you are cared for and you belong. I know this feeling deep within me, to have been orphaned and alone, and then all of a sudden you find a home when and where you least expect it. Only a month ago, Kabita and Jayanti were weaving blankets in the cold dry mountain air of Jumla, and Kanchi was playing with her baby goat. None of them had any idea they would be

158

sold into another life. Yet that cruel plan had been interrupted, by fate: by Dilly dragging me to see a Hindi cinema in Bichia, by his decision to take the rough track by the river rather than our usual route, and by Hira Prashad's sense.

How life can change in a moment. Is that fate or chance?

PART IV

THE WARNING

NINETEEN

ira Prashad's chains seemed twice as heavy to me now. Ever since I had seen the wild elephant's tracks before the monsoon, I wondered, why does that large bull run free and my tusker is chained? I began to apologize every night I set the choker chain around his right front leg and again every morning when I awoke to release his shackles and take him to graze and drink by the river.

How could I chain my brother? There must be another way.

Indra nodded toward the grove, where a thin stream of incense curled out above it like a snake. "Wait here, Indra," I said. "I'll be right back." I had a good idea that my father was praying for insight—for which of our pressing issues, I did not know. He had been restless since the conservator-*sahib*'s visit. He even suggested that we had "no time for Tihar," the second-biggest holiday of the year.

163

When I entered the grove, several candles burned in a large triangle. My father was bowed in prayer to Ban Devi in the center. Incense wafted around him. Suddenly his eyes shot open and looked at me. My father, the shaman, did not look peaceful in his trance, as usual. His teeth were clenched, and his gaze cut through me.

"Nandu, I have had a vision that is everything I had hoped to never see. We must act quickly. You, Indra, and Dilly must go with your elephants up to the Chisapani guard post and, if necessary, north to the Bheri River Valley. Let us hope that you find our rhinos safe. Prepare to leave tomorrow."

"But why not Ramji and some of the older drivers?" I asked.

"Because I trust you." My father's expression seemed so sad that I did not press further. A part of me glowed that he believed in us, the youngest in the stable. Maybe he did see me in his place, someday, and not just because of his gout.

I left to tell Dilly and Indra. Then I borrowed Dilly's bicycle to go tell Father Autry that I would miss my lesson. When I told him the news, Father Autry asked if there was room for one more.

"I don't want to be a burden, Nandu, but there is a species of fern that is supposed to grow in the Bheri Valley that I would like to add to my collection." My tutor's passion was the study of ferns.

"We would be honored to have you, Father-*sahib*. You will be another pair of eyes for us, too."

My father was happy for Father Autry to travel with us as well. He trusted us, but having Father Autry along gave him more peace of mind. I know he preferred to come himself, but his gout made it hard for him to walk even from the gazebo to his bungalow.

We left at dawn and by late afternoon we reached the Chisapani guard post at the mouth of the gorge. We found only one guard on duty. When we asked where the others were, he nodded across the river at the *raksi* stall. He said they would probably be back before dark, when the old boatman made his last trip across the Great Sand Bar River for the night. A dugout boat full of tipsy guards would be dangerous passengers. Most Nepalis do not know how to swim.

We spent the night at the guard post, camped on the veranda, but the other guards never returned. In the morning, we decided not to wait for them. We would head up the ridge and into the Bheri Valley on our own. By noon, we were halfway up the trail. Hira Prashad seemed to be enjoying the trek himself. Elephants are wonderful climbers and can scale steep hillsides with their round, flat feet.

"Nandu. Have I ever told you the story of Hannibal crossing the Alps with his warrior elephants?" asked Father Autry.

"I have heard of Hannibal," I said. "But not this story."

"The general Hannibal from Carthage commanded a large army of elephants, Nandu. They crossed the Alps for a surprise attack on the Roman Empire."

"Did they win?"

"Only a few elephants survived the harsh climb, I'm afraid. But Hannibal's army did defeat the Romans."

"I am glad our elephants are not used this way now, Father-*sahib*. They are such kind and gentle beings. It hurts me to think of them to be used as killers." A part of me felt our use was wrong, too. At least, on this day they were working to help us protect their fellow wild creatures, the rhinos.

We reached the top of the ridge and paused to enjoy the view and have a drink of water from our canteens. We started our descent to the Bheri Valley, climbing down the mountain and keeping our eyes open on the outcrop of rocks.

"Eureka!" Father Autry had sighted what he thought was his spleenwort fern.

I tried to be happy for him, but I think Father Autry could sense I was still upset. He could read my mood like Hira Prashad. I could not shake the thought of elephants killing enemy soldiers and being killed in battle. The image of the villager about to spear the Baba's tiger came back to me. Why do people tame some wild animals but then kill them the moment they behave as is in their nature? People make no attempt to understand animals, only to control them.

The sun was sinking over the *sal* forest when we reached the first guard post at the entrance to the Bheri Valley. I had expected the three guards stationed there to be waiting for us, especially since we had arrived on elephants, easily seen at a distance. I jumped off Hira Prashad and clambered up the steps of the post and looked around. It was empty.

Dilly held his hand over the fire pit. "Nandu, no one has burned wood here for days."

Now we knew that what we feared was, in fact, the truth. Nobody was protecting the rhinos.

We dismounted and made camp for the night. In the morning we would go out and search. Indra and Dilly started to cook a curry made from dried strips of goat meat and bitter melon we had brought as a special treat to share with the guards.

After dinner, Father Autry told us stories about his life growing up on a farm in Arkansas. When he was twelve years old, he had a donkey named Socrates. "Donkeys are very smart," he said, "especially my Socrates. Sometimes I would sing to my donkey and he would pretend to like it."

I lay down by the fire, imagining my beloved tutor as a boy my age riding a donkey. We were about to go to sleep in our bedrolls when Hira Prashad started to rumble.

"Maybe it is one of the rhinos," said Indra.

Dilly put out the fire. It was pitch-black. In the quiet, gunshots rang through the air. We sat in tense silence, waiting for more sounds, but we heard nothing more. It was too dark to investigate now. Too dangerous. We would have to wait until morning.

I started awake several times. Then the first thing I saw in the light of dawn was a kettle of vultures circling in the sky. A second warning. I had shivers as I began to look for Hira Prashad. It was not from the chilly air, even though I was barefoot and without a coat. It was the gnawing fear of what I knew was out there. A jungle that once felt like a place to discover beautiful creatures now began to fill me with terror in what I would find.

I told myself that perhaps it was a cow that had wandered into the reserve and died, but we were miles from the nearest village. Dilly struggled to ignite the log from last night's fire to make tea, but it was too damp from the heavy morning dew. Overhead, another stream of vultures flapped through the mist. I could not wait to get moving.

We saddled the elephants as soon as we could find them in the grassland where we had left them for the night. We approached the valley bottom to discover a great wheel of circling birds. Hira Prashad and Man Kali raised their trunks over the reeds and led us to a small opening by the Bheri River.

The dense grass gave way to a nightmare. Hundreds of vultures were perched on the ground or along the wide branches of the silk cotton trees by the riverbank. At the base of one tree was a rhino bleeding from its head. I was hoping it was still alive. But I knew that no living rhino would allow two elephants to approach it from behind. The vultures had not yet touched the flesh.

"We are too late. The poachers have carried off their prize," Father Autry said. The rhino's horn had been cut off the beautiful creature's face. I felt the anger and nausea rise, almost at the same time. It was the way I felt when I saw Pradhan's face. I had to keep myself from vomiting or shouting, or both.

Dilly pointed to the bullet holes that entered the rhino's skull and chest.

"Nandu, we should dig out one of the bullets and take it back to give to *Subba-sahib*. He can show it to the police," Dilly said.

"No, Dilly, we will need to use our hand axes to remove it. Without the warden present, we would be in trouble if we touched the rhino."

I lost the little control I had over my emotions and started to tremble. Father Autry put his hand on my shoulder and spoke softly to us. "Drivers," he said, "when something terrible has happened, like this, our first job is to remain as calm as possible. We need to stay clearheaded and come up with a plan."

Dilly and Indra nodded.

"Let us return to Thakurdwara and alert *Subba-sahib* and the warden," Father Autry said. "He will know what to do." By *he*, I knew he meant *Subba-sahib*, not the warden or his new assistant, Ganesh Lal, the wildlife *expert*.

"What evil people would do such a thing to a rhino? Where are the guards?"

169

Then it occurred to me. What if the guards up here were being paid off by the poachers? Why had they left their post and the rhinos unprotected?

"Do you think whoever did this is still nearby?" asked Dilly.

"They probably left quickly," said Father Autry. "It doesn't help that even one rhino horn sold to a smuggler is equal to a year's wage for a poaching gang. The best we can do is to go back and bring more guards. Or maybe an army unit. We will send a message to Kathmandu, even if the warden does not."

"Let's hurry," said Dilly.

I knew that Father Autry's plan was the right one, but part of me didn't want to go. I wanted to stay and keep the vultures away from the body. I would beat them with a stick if they came close, but I knew this was pointless. The vultures were doing their jobs as scavengers. Now it was time to do ours.

"Come on, Nandu. We have poachers to catch," said Father Autry.

"Yes, we do."

TWENTY

The elephants climbed faster than I had ever seen them do before. It was like Hira Prashad and Man Kali were in a race to the top. At the peak, they were exhausted and needed to rest and graze for a few hours. Dilly and I unsaddled our elephants, then Indra walked them down the hillside to keep an eye on them while they grazed.

The Borderlands stretched below us. From here the world looked peaceful and lush, but somewhere under that green blanket lurked poachers. I could not shake the image of the rhino surrounded by hundreds of vultures. It had been horrible to see Pradhan dead and mutilated, but this killing was even worse. Pradhan was old and would not live much longer on this earth. This rhino was a young female who may have even had calves. Her death was unholy, a sin against nature.

Even the king had agreed with me when I saved a young mother tigress from his shot during a Royal Hunt. Such a killing would be a kind of crime . . . and yet, it was all I could think of. I could not escape the image of the second dead rhino in my head. There was no room for anything else. First Pradhan, and now this new one.

We were sitting in silence, off the trail behind some boulders. "I am sorry we did not get to search for more of your ferns, Father-*sahib*," I said.

"Think nothing of it. We are rightly focused on the terrible task at hand. But I thank you for mentioning it, Nandu."

Dilly motioned to us to join him behind a boulder. He held his finger to his lips. A chill ran through me. Father Autry and I scampered next to him and heard a whistle. It sounded like a male *chir* pheasant calling to his females.

A group of five men approached less than a quarter mile away. The older two fanned out just below our hiding spot, clutching their homemade bows. The leader whistled again, imitating the sound of the birds. They were hunting. If these were our poachers, I saw no rifles. Had they hidden their weapons?

The group of hunters passed by without making another sound. Far behind them followed a small band of women and children moving silently. They carried their baskets and wore simple frocks and scarves on their heads. From our hiding spot, we watched until they were out of earshot.

"Raute!" Father Autry declared. "I thought they were only a legend. Do you realize we have just seen Nepal's last remaining band of hunter-gatherers?"

"Do you think they shot the rhino and took its horn?" I asked. "I didn't see anyone carrying a rifle."

"No, it would not be them, Nandu," said Dilly. "Ramji says they only hunt what they eat. They live on monkeys and ground birds. Mostly peacocks and *chir* pheasants I would guess."

"I agree. These are not our rhino poachers," said my tutor.

"They only hunt with bows and arrows, but they are deadly with them," said Dilly. "And they are excellent trackers, better than any of us. They say a Raute can sneak up to a sleeping tiger and touch its nose without ever waking it."

"Maybe they have seen the poachers!" I said. "Perhaps we should go ask them?"

"They are long gone, Nandu," said Dilly, "and they would disappear into the boulders if we came close. They avoid anyone who is not in their tribe."

We sat back down and waited for Indra and the elephants. My thoughts returned to the poor rhino. I wished we had rangers with us who might be carrying a radio. It would take us so long to get a message to the king to ask for help, and he was the only person with the power to push the guards into action.

We made *chapattis* with tomato pickle for lunch. The sun was climbing and a half hour had passed. I got up to stretch my legs and look for Indra. When I glanced down the trail from behind the boulder I noticed a boy about my age hobbling along. He was a Raute, dressed in tattered clothes. He stopped to lean on a crutch fashioned from tree limbs. Then he took two more steps, tumbled, and let out a soft whimper as he collapsed on the trail.

I called Father Autry for help. The boy grabbed for his bow and arrows. But I was fast and kicked them away from him. Father Autry got hold of his arms and restrained him. I did not know what to do, so I put my hand on the boy's racing heart. When it began to slow, I took one of his hands from Father Autry and put it on my chest. The boy slumped into Father Autry's lap.

We offered the boy *chapattis* and tomato pickle, motioning for him to eat. But he refused to take anything. He spoke a few words we could not make out. We released him and he grabbed the *chapattis*, hunger overcoming fear. The boy spoke only a few words of Nepali. He kept saying, "My family. My family. You see? You see?" while pointing to my eyes and then the trail. That must have been who first passed us.

Father Autry examined his injury.

"This unfortunate boy has a broken leg," Father Autry explained. "That is why the tribe had to leave him behind."

No, Father-sahib, they did not have to leave him, they must have decided to leave him. What is it about families? First my family, then the Jumlis, and now this boy. Why did they not cherish us?

"We have to take him back to the stable to be treated by Doctor-*sahib*," I said. Our veterinarian was also our human doctor in areas my father's shaman skill could not cover.

Indra returned with the elephants, and the boy tried

to get up but he could not move. He slumped back down to the ground. Father Autry reached into his bag and pulled out cashew nuts and handed them to the young Raute. He ate every one. We gave him a canteen full of water but he did not know how to drink from it. Indra unscrewed the lid and showed him what to do. The boy finished the entire canteen. He must have been left without water or food.

Now the problem was how to carry him back to the stable. I tried to lift him, but he made himself heavy. Then I looked over at Hira Prashad, nodding to my tusker.

Please help me, brother elephant.

Hira Prashad came over and gently sniffed the boy and caressed his head with his trunk. The boy giggled. He probably did not expect the elephant to be so gentle. Indra quickly picked up some jungle vines and branches to fashion a makeshift cover to fit over his leg for our journey. We helped him up slowly.

"Pasar!" I commanded. Hira Prashad lowered himself and sprawled to one side to allow us to load the boy on the saddle. The boy laughed at this. You could tell he was tough. I noticed his body was covered in scabs and sores. I had been left like him, too—alone in the jungle. At least this boy would know why. I would never know.

"What will we do with this Jungle Boy, Nandu?" Indra asked. That is what he called him, the Jungle Boy.

"He needs to have this leg examined. I can see the bone

breaking the skin. He is lucky not to be dead already," said my tutor.

At first the rocking of Hira Prashad was painful for the Raute. I looked back and Father Autry was cradling the Jungle Boy's head in his hands. Then I realized our Raute might never have seen a white man before either. No wonder Father Autry had given him such a fright.

Everyone was worn-out by now. We still had at least five hours to go before we reached the stable. No one was more exhausted than this poor Raute. Only Father Autry remained energized and beaming. New experiences were like an elixir to him, and meeting the Raute seemed much more exciting than finding ten new species of fern.

"Do you realize the Raute have lived this way for thousands of years? That band passing was like watching the Stone Age come to life!"

I wanted to disagree, but I only nodded. In the Stone Age the people would have killed for food, not out of greed and cruelty. I would wait to bring it up for our next lesson about evolution, using it as evidence that humans have actually *devolved* since then.

Father Autry admired the Raute for living as nomads, with no village. "The Raute wander the foothills and low mountains of western Nepal. But few anthropologists have ever really had a chance to study their ways. They stay away from civilization, I have been told," said Father Autry.

"*Subba-sahib* says they know a lot about jungle medicine and make much use of the *chiuri* fruit and seeds. It is their lifeblood, and they worship *chiuri* trees," I said.

"You know, Nandu, just like animals can be classified as endangered, so can rare tribes. There might not be more than two hundred Raute left in the hills, scattered among a few wandering groups. They have their own language and customs. When they are gone, the world will be poorer," my tutor said. "We still have much to learn from groups like the Raute, Nandu."

Again, I did not agree but said nothing. When I am angry with the world, it is better to be silent. To leave one of their own behind, with a broken leg and no food, what could be crueler than that? They were no better than the villagers who wanted to spear the Babu's tiger.

After the first hour, Jungle Boy fell into a deep sleep from the gentle rocking of the elephant, or from Father Autry's lullaby. Maybe it was the same one he sang to Socrates the donkey, back when he was a boy.

TWENTY-ONE

The walls of Mr. Dhungel's office were covered with large framed photographs of His Majesty the King and Her Majesty the Queen. I noticed a smaller one with the warden taken from the side, bowing low in front of His Majesty, about to receive a medal. I recognized the warden from his thick, black-rimmed glasses. This ceremony must have been the high point of his life. Now the news we were about to share could lead to that medal being stripped from him.

"Dhungel-*sahib*, we must send an armed patrol right away to protect the Bheri Valley rhinos. They have poached one rhino, and will surely poach the others. The guards have fled their post, so there is nothing to stop them," my father declared.

Mr. Dhungel's glasses slid down his nose; it happened when he was excited. Then he threw up his hands and shook his head vigorously. "Why do you bring me such unwelcome news, *Subba-sahib*?"

Do something, you idiot! I thought.

My hope that the warden-*sahib* would take bold action disappeared.

Ganesh Lal, the wildlife expert, who had been standing in the corner, stepped forward to speak. But the warden waved him off with a hand gesture. He stepped back again.

"Why did you not bring back the bullet, Nandu?" He quizzed me like I had done something wrong. "How can we be sure that this rhino died by the poachers' hands? Maybe it was a coincidence and they were out hunting deer or a wild pig for the pot? This could have been an old rhino. Yes, that is what I believe."

"But we *saw* the bullet holes, Warden-*sahib*," I pleaded. "This was a healthy adult female. And they cut off her horn. They were *not* deer hunting."

My father put his hand on my shoulder to calm me. I was in danger of being scolded by the dung beetle for my impudence. But the warden did something far worse.

"Do not tell anyone about this," the warden said. "We will say the rhino died from natural causes. Porcupines chewed up the horn before we could reach the site and retrieve it. There will be too much trouble if I report a poaching incident. I will ensure that the guards return to their post and prevent any further losses. Leave this to me."

I looked over at Ganesh Lal, who met my gaze but said nothing. His lips parted as if to speak, but then perhaps he thought the better of it and stared at his feet. That is what most adults do when there is trouble and action has to be taken. They stare at their feet.

My heart sank. Nothing would be done, and all the rhinos between here and Chisapani were likely to meet the same bloody fate. I could barely lift my head all the way back to camp. Why was the warden so reluctant to investigate? Was he afraid to have the king's medal taken away? I was convinced there was a spy among us. Someone who could bribe the guards and easily get to the rhinos. Perhaps Ganesh Lal. But he seemed too incompetent to be involved. Perhaps the game warden—but he was even more foolish than Ganesh Lal. Perhaps Mr. Rijal, the conservator, but he seemed a decent man, if not the most energetic official. I did not know. A darker thought occurred to me then. What if the spy was from our stable? A driver. That could not be . . . but why did my father not trust the other drivers? The images of Pradhan, and then the man on the shore of the Great Sand Bar River, came rushing back to me. Was the man in the blue sneakers the ringleader? What about the man in Bichia selling elephant ivory in the middle of the bazaar? He was so brazen. I tried to puzzle it out in my head, thinking of the clues we had before us.

I had more questions than answers. And now the only people I could turn to for answers were my father, Father Autry, Dilly, and Indra.

We arrived to find that Kabita, Jayanti, and Kanchi had prepared a soak for the bath to restore tired bones. "You need to revive your spirits," said Kanchi to our newest orphan, the Raute. She gestured as she spoke, creating a pantomime with her fingers. "We picked herbs from the jungle, mint and lemongrass, and mixed it with a powder we use in Jumla." She pretended to pick leaves with her fingers and mix them. Then she held it up for him to smell.

Father Autry and I carefully lifted Jungle Boy into a shallow tub. He was wearing my undershorts, and I had a fresh set of pants and shirt ready for him.

"Be careful with his leg, Nandu," my tutor advised.

Kabita and Jayanti went back to their weaving on Tulsi's loom to start on some proper clothes for our guest. Kanchi stayed and helped us fetch more warm water to add to his bath as it cooled.

That night I slept on a mat on the floor and gave Jungle Boy my cot. He did not wake up until daybreak thanks to Father Autry, who had ground up a sleeping pill in the rice and milk and raisins we fed our patient.

At sunrise, Doctor-*sahib* arrived at camp carrying his vet bag. He had come to check on the elephants. Little did he know we had another, more pressing job for him.

"Greetings, Nandu. How are our little jumbos? Gaining weight?"

"They are all fine, Doctor-*sahib*. But please take a look at someone who needs your help," I said. I wondered if the vet had talked to the warden already. Now was not the time to bring up the dead rhino. Not yet.

I led him to the cot where the boy was resting surrounded by people. Father Autry, Kanchi, and Dilly were sitting with Rita. Kanchi had brought a hairbrush and was gently brushing his hair. The boy did not seem to mind the attention, which probably distracted him from the pain in his leg.

We tried to use sign language to explain who this stranger was and that he was a doctor there to examine his fracture. The boy seemed wary and his thin body tensed. I held out my bare leg to show him how painless this would be. Doctor-*sahib* pretended to be giving me an exam. I pointed to him and Doctor-*sahib* and to his leg and put his hand to my heart again and he relaxed. I think he understood me.

We carefully removed yesterday's wrapping to keep the flies off the exposed bone. Doctor-*sahib*'s eyes widened. He cleaned the wound gently and replaced the covering. Doctor-*sahib* nodded to us to step outside.

"No. Stay here." Kanchi spoke up. "If you leave, it will scare him. He does not understand us, Doctor-*sahib*, so speak in a soft tone and tell us what we should do."

"This is very dangerous. If an infection gets in the bone tissue we might have to amputate his leg. We can give him antibiotics, but we have no choice. The bone has partially healed but at the wrong angle. If we do not reset it, he will remain a cripple."

"How do we reset the bone, Doctor-*sahib*?" I asked, though in reality, I did not want to know.

Doctor-*sahib* practically whispered. "I will have to break it again, Nandu; there is no choice."

When it was time, Father Autry stood on one side of the boy and I was on the other. We had already given him an injection of painkillers, and the Raute was babbling. When the doctor signaled he was ready, I felt my head start to spin and the nausea rise in my throat.

I staggered out of the room. I heard a sharp moan and a horrible sound as the vomit came out of me. I felt ashamed of my weakness for pain.

When I came back, Doctor-*sahib* said, "It is all right, Nandu. The worst is over now. When you left, Kanchi took your place and held his hand through the whole thing. She did not even flinch. Thank you, Kanchi," he said.

Kanchi never looked up at Doctor-*sahib* or me. She did not need the praise. Instead she wiped Jungle Boy's face with a soft towel.

Doctor-*sahib* then made a cast from plaster of paris to protect the leg while it healed. When the boy finally awoke, he looked down at his leg and let out a high, bloodcurdling shriek. He did not utter a sound for the next two days.

Kanchi stayed at his side. We all took turns visiting him, and although he probably understood almost nothing I said to him, he returned my smile. He knew we all cared, and that was all that mattered.

Only Kanchi managed to communicate with the boy through a combination of drawing pictures, sign language, and the few Nepali words the boy spoke. She pieced together his story and told it to us.

"Nandu, he is from a small clan that wanders the forests north of the Borderlands. In winter, when it grows too cold to hunt in the highlands, the Raute drop down from the mountains to where it is warmer. They eat birds, turtles, and monkeys, really anything they can shoot or snare."

"How did he get injured and why did they leave him?" I asked.

"He was crossing over a ravine on a slippery log. He fell and broke his leg. The clan camped by the ravine for two weeks." The boy understood at least part of what Kanchi was telling us. He held up seven fingers and seven fingers again to show us the number of days they tried to help him, but still he could not walk. He used his two fingers to show us him trying to stand and then falling over.

"The clan leader is his father," she said. "When they had

hunted all the game out of the area, he had no choice but to leave his son behind. They did leave him some food and water."

"He must have been desperate to catch up with them, the way he was hobbling up the trail," Father Autry said.

"It must have been very painful to keep walking on his broken leg," I told Kanchi.

"I am so glad you brought him here, Nandu. He would have died."

Kanchi called him *Maila*, the name we give to a middle brother, just as Kanchi, her nickname, means *little sister*. "Nandu, he is younger than Dilly and Indra but older than you. It is kinder to call him Maila than Jungle Boy."

With all the food we brought him and the antibiotics Doctor-*sahib* left behind, Maila began to heal. He started to laugh and smile. Kanchi had brought him out of his shell even though they could only speak a few words together. I wondered if Kanchi had told Maila that her father had abandoned her, too, sent her away with a bandit for a few sacks of rice. But then I thought it was probably an emotion they shared without even having to say the words.

TWENTY-TWO

The festival of Tihar is the holiday we look forward to all year long. This year, I had forgotten entirely about it on our trip to Chisapani and the Bheri River Valley. As it happened, we had returned just in time for the festival.

We call it *Tihar*, but the Tharu and people across the border in India call it *Diwali*. It is all the same holiday, though. It means the Festival of Light. During Tihar or Diwali, even the poorest people put oil into tiny clay cups and add a simple candlewick. These tiny lamps are scattered everywhere. When the wicks are lit at dusk, it looks like a swarm of lightning bugs hovering around our world.

The death of the rhino still weighed on my heart, but the festival helped put a flicker of light into my spirit. Mine were not the only spirits lifted. The holiday asks us to honor what we take for granted, and reminds us to appreciate all we have. In Nepal, we honor the animals that we usually ignore or chase

186

away, such as the house crow and the village dogs. Every Tihar, I ride with my elephant to the grasslands and leave fruit and saffron rice for the *dhole*, my *dhole*, who protected me when I was a baby, alone in the jungle.

While I was in the jungle doing my ritual, Dilly had gone to a nearby village to buy fireworks for the two of us. I had given him thirty rupees and told him I wanted the special bottle rockets that burst into bright colors. I double-checked that I had them in my satchel before we left for the village.

Rita, Kabita, Jayanti, Kanchi, and I took off for Thakurdwara to watch everyone prepare for Tihar. The girls sang songs from the mountain tribes along the way. I wondered if during Tihar they missed their families even more. "What is Tihar like in your village, Kabita?" I asked.

"Sometimes, like this year when there was no monsoon, we do not even have enough wheat flour left over to make *sel roti*. There is no oil for lamps, either."

"I cannot imagine Tihar without eating *sel roti*," I said. It is a special sweet bread that we only eat once a year.

"You eat like kings in the Borderlands," said Jayanti. "Even the dogs here are better fed than some children in our village." The girls were no longer as skinny as when we first met. The cuts on their wrists and ankles had long healed. Kabita had quietly told me that their legs were bound that day in the wagon because Kanchi had tried to run away.

"Do you miss Jumla, Kanchi?" Rita asked.

"I miss my two goats and the lamb I looked after. But now I have Laxmi Kali, who needs me. And Nani. I have you as my *didi*, Rita, and Nandu and Indra and Dilly as my *daju*." She started to sing again and the girls joined in.

We reached the fields where Dilly was waiting with Indra and a few boys from the village. I unloaded half of the firecrackers and bottle rockets from my satchel. Indra lit the firecrackers and tossed them on the ground. They went off like small gunshots. The girls shrieked.

While Dilly arranged six of the twelve bottle rockets I had purchased for the festival, Rita gave each of the girls sparklers.

"What do we do with these, *didi*?" Kanchi asked Rita. I lit Rita's sparkler, and she twirled it round Kanchi's head, making an orbit of stars around her. "You are no longer a girl from Jumla. Kanchi, you are a princess from Kathmandu!"

Kanchi took the sparkler from Rita and twirled it over her own head to make a halo. "No, I am a *mahout* from the Borderlands who rides her elephant, Laxmi Kali," she sang.

"Jayanti, Kabita, watch this!" shouted Dilly over the noise of the firecrackers Indra had lit. I had noticed lately that Dilly was always trying to get Jayanti's attention, even if he tried to hide it by including her sister.

Dilly put a match to the fuses on the first three rockets, and they shot into the sky, hissing like giant pythons. They exploded, shattering pieces of emerald, sapphire, and ruby light over the field. The next three rockets shot off and showered us in flakes of gold and silver. Kabita, Jayanti, and Kanchi had never seen fireworks. The screamed and laughed, and their eyes flashed, reflecting the fiery sparkles against the black sky.

"Dilly, we should save the rest of the fireworks for tomorrow," I said. "We do not want to use them all up tonight."

"You are spoiling the fun, Nandu," he said. "We have plenty of fireworks."

"I am not spoiling the fun."

"Yes, you are," said Kanchi. "Keep going, Dilly!"

My face flushed hot. I had not meant to ruin the night. I wanted to be sure we had *enough* fun for the next evening, which was the real Tihar celebration. I was quiet as we walked back to the stable. I did not like Dilly talking to me that way, and showing off to impress Jayanti.

The fog was so thick the next morning, I could barely make out the tethering area. It was only fifty feet from the edge of the barracks, but I could not see the elephants. When I reached Hira Prashad's post, he was gone. He had slipped his chains in the night. I had set them loose like *Subba-sahib* had told me to do in case the wild bull returned. "Indra, Dilly, come quick! Hira Prashad has gone. Indra, tell *Subba-sahib*. Dilly and I will go on foot and you can catch up with us on the elephants."

I raced back to the barracks to grab my satchel. I threw in it some *kuchis* to lure my tusker back. Then we followed Hira Pra-shad's tracks, bending low as we ran to watch his path on the ground. Luckily, he kept to the dirt track, so we could easily see his enormous footprints.

Soon we found a fresh pile of his steaming droppings. "Dilly, he must be close."

"He is headed to Lalmati. I wonder if he is going to cross the river there."

Was he going to meet the other tusker?

The sun was rising, burning off the top layer of fog, which hovered like wisps of gray cotton over the jungle. Still, on the ground, we could barely see a hundred feet in front of us. After almost two hours of trailing him, we caught a glimpse of Hira Prashad, sticking out of the fog, but only his rear end, before he vanished back into the forest. We followed as best we could straight into the Lalmati grassland.

A roar echoed across the northern rim. I had never heard such a sound. A battle cry! Hira Prashad roared back, and the sounds filled the valley around us. Soon we heard beneath the roars the squeaks and rumbles of more elephants. As if nature were on our side, the fog lifted like the velvet curtain at the Hindi cinema, and the open area in front of us came into view. At the far end, maybe three hundred feet away, were twenty wild elephants. In the middle of the grassland was the giant bull who had rushed through our camp weeks ago.

Facing off, his ears spread wide in a threatening posture, was my Hira Prashad, ready to defend his family.

"Dilly, that tusker could kill him."

"We cannot do anything, Nandu. This fight is between them."

The two bulls roared and lunged for each other. They slapped each other with their trunks. The tusks of the wild bull grazed Hira Prashad. They backed away from each other for a moment, then the wild bull charged again. He was stronger, but Hira Prashad was more agile. He dodged the wild male's tusks, then turned, scraping his own tusks across the face of the wild male, who let out a bloodcurdling cry of pain.

The earth shook underneath my feet from the power of the clashing giants. I could not watch. I sat down, using my satchel as a mat, and tucked my face into my hands. My tusker was going to die.

I flashed back to when I had first seen Hira Prashad, when he was being starved to death by the two elephant handlers. The Python, the wealthy local landlord who had employed the men, wanted my tusker's ivory. Then we rescued him, only for him to end up fighting for his life, in this same grassland where he had saved mine from the earthquake. I prayed for another tremor to shake the trees and make the elephants run for safety.

At last I stood and saw the rival bull lunge at Hira Prashad. My elephant quickly moved out of his way. But he would tire soon, and the more powerful male would gore my tusker and that would be the end. I wanted to run to get between them to plead with them to stop, but I knew I would be trampled.

My thoughts raced as I tried to think of something I could do. I sat down in despair. Then suddenly I felt the lump I had been sitting on. In the satchel were some firecrackers and a few cherry bombs that I had stuffed into my pack last night.

"Dilly, do you have your lighter?" I shouted.

I took out my slingshot, which I always kept for protection, and the fireworks. Dilly nodded, without even having to speak.

I positioned the firecrackers in my slingshot. "Okay, light the fuses," I said.

Dilly lit the first one. I fired it toward the wild bull. He turned to face me.

"The cherry bomb, Dilly!"

I shot the cherry bomb next. It exploded at the bull's feet. He raised his trunk and spread his ears, like he was about to charge. I had his full attention and his herd's, too. The females and young jumbos panicked and ran back into the cover of the jungle, distracting him.

The roaring and trumpeting resumed. The two males lunged at each other. The hollow clatter of tusk against tusk rang across the grasslands.

"Dilly, let's try a rocket," I said. I was desperate. The bottle rocket shot into the air and exploded, but the bull elephants ignored the confetti of colors and kept attacking each other.

When I turned around, the elephants from our stable were standing right behind us. They had moved in as silently as ghosts. My father was by my side. I was never so relieved to see him.

"*Subba-sahib*, what do we do?"

"Nothing, Nandu. We must wait and pray. This bull is too dangerous for any of us to approach. The fireworks helped us find you. We came straight to the noise."

I knelt to the ground.

Ban Devi, please protect Hira Prashad. And do not let him kill this bull. No one should die.

The bulls lunged at each other one more time. Then they both stopped. Our goddess had heard me.

"Look, *Subba-sahib*, they are exhausted. They have taken measure of each other. It is a standoff. Maybe they will both retreat to their herds," Ramji said.

The two tuskers did not move for five minutes more. I strained to hear their conversation through the soles of my bare feet. I thought if I closed my eyes, I might see an image, a clue to what they were saying.

"Nandu, put your hand on Prem Kali's trunk and on Punti Kali's, too," my father instructed me. "They are talking to the two males, of this I am sure, even if we cannot hear anything. I believe they are saying in their language, 'Stop fighting, you are brothers, not rivals. You must both protect our herd.'"

The wild herd reappeared from the edge of the forest.

An old female trumpeted and turned away, as if she had had enough of the spectacle. The wild tusker drifted off silently and followed her into the jungle.

I climbed up on Bhim Prashad and sat behind my father, who calmly directed his elephant to turn toward the stable. Our other elephants followed. I was afraid to look, but when I turned, there was Hira Prashad following us at a distance, his trunk searching the air and finally dropping. Peace had been reached. At least for now.

TWENTY-THREE

My peaceful kingdom was becoming a battleground. There was already a battle between our stable and the poachers, and now, on top of that, a war between two giant tuskers for control over the Borderlands herds—wild and domestic. "*Subba-sahib*, the two bulls fight when they should be allies. What if the poachers turn from rhinos to elephants?"

"I think that bull and our Hira Prashad are safe for now, Nandu. Rhino horn is worth much more to them than elephant ivory. But we need to step up our protection and push the warden. He is new and naïve. And Ganesh Lal seems like he has no clue either about what to do."

Ten days had passed since we returned from the Bheri Valley. To the best of our knowledge, the warden had done nothing. My father sent word to his contact in the Royal Palace, asking if there had been any activity at the guard posts in question, and his contact had answered that "everything is as usual."

My father was more agitated than I had ever seen him. He hated being part of another man's lie—especially when that lie was the result of cowardice.

My father gathered us together in the tethering area in the early hours of the morning to speak to us drivers.

"It is our duty to go check on the rhinos in the Bheri River Valley, and on the return, travel along the Great Sand Bar River near Lalmati to locate as many rhinos as we can. We are their defenders now. We will report our census numbers to the authorities. I will take five elephants and ten drivers with me. We leave tomorrow."

"*Subba-sahib,*" I said. "Will Hira Prashad's wounds be a problem?"

"No," my father said firmly. "He is far tougher than that."

Father Autry came to see us off. He would not join us this time, but he had offered to stay behind with Maila, Rita, and the girls.

"Good luck, Nandu," he said. "Let us hope you find them." I waved to him and to what now looked like a flock of children surrounding him: Maila, Rita, Kabita, Jayanti, and Kanchi. They waved back, their arms flapping like wings.

It took us two days to reach the Bheri Valley. I had to work to keep my mind from conjuring images of the worst we might find. We climbed switchbacks up the steep Siwalik slopes, five elephants, single file, in silence. I thought of Hannibal scaling the Alps as we made our way up to the ridge. We would be an army to defend the lives of the rhinos. But in truth I felt powerless to truly save them. To wait two days to answer a question of life or death is an eternity. Time slows down. Each second ticks away at hope.

I imagined running into the poachers surrounding a rhino. Except this time, like Hannibal, we were riding the king of Nepal's war elephants. I pictured Hira Prashad with armor on his face and trunk, charging the poachers, straight at their rifles aimed our way—trampling them before they could shoot. Over the long hours, my story grew more and more vivid.

We would reach the rhinos in time. We had to.

The guard post was again deserted when we arrived.

Where have the rangers gone? This is their duty. Why has the warden not sent Ganesh Lal to oversee these posts? He is useless back at the warden's office. He should be out in the field, near the rhinos.

It was late October, so I was surprised to hear so few birds singing. Had life left the Bheri Valley? At least there were no vultures circling, a good sign. We made camp and allowed the elephants to graze freely.

"We will spread out and search the valley from one end to the other, starting tomorrow," my father instructed. "Take rest, drivers, tomorrow will be a long day."

I was on edge. Each time I fell asleep, violent images woke me. In my nightmares, the poachers fired cannons at our war elephants. We were thrown as our brave warrior elephants dropped to the ground and died at our feet.

Real life, though, is never like nightmares. It is often worse. Just after dawn, the elephants led us to the first carcass, or what remained of it, a few hundred feet from where we had found the first dead rhino almost two weeks ago. All that was left was a piece of the large skull the hyenas could not drag off. I took deep breaths so that my emotions would not overpower me. We had to stay focused on our quest to count their numbers and report their deaths. In this way, the palace would have to take heed, even if it was too late to save these rhinos.

"Now I am worried about the rhinos between Chisapani and Lalmati," my father said. "We must go there quickly. Let us not spend more time here. We will come back to the Bheri with the commanding officers." My father turned to face us all, strong and angry. "To Lalmati, drivers!"

The elephants descended the ridge single file. Four miles below the Chisapani guard post, five more rhino skulls and a few scattered bones, picked clean, littered the earth. The vultures had long finished their work, so we had to rely on the elephants and our own eyes.

With the discovery of each new carcass in the tall grass, another piece of me sank deeper. I did not think I was capable of such sadness.

Hira Prashad found them first, indicating we were nearby with a deep, mournful rumble. Elephants have human emotions, or we humans have some fraction of theirs. I believe the latter is closer to the truth.

Every other mile we found another poached rhino. The same scene: only the skull left but with clear signs where the nasal bones would have been, the signs of chopping with an ax. There were no footprints or blue canvas sneakers, or any clues as to who did this. Too much time had passed.

I wondered if I came upon a poacher in the act and had a rifle in my hands, would I have shot those people dead? Would I have fired at the boy who set the snares and was part of their gang? At that moment, I am afraid I would have had no trouble pulling the trigger. These people were murderers.

"If only the warden would have sent more guards," I blurted out.

My father said nothing. When he is deeply upset he does not talk.

We found eight more rhinos, or what was left of them, before dark. We marked where they had been killed on a map. The last rhinos had been shot near Lalmati. *Subba-sahib* thought they had been dead for a week or more. Searching along the Great Sand Bar River, we found old bones of ten more rhinos that had been scattered by hyenas. These must have been poached since May, when Pradhan was killed. It is why our count with Ganesh Lal could not locate the fifty rhinos we thought lived in the reserve. Some were already killed, but they were shot too far from our stable to hear the poachers' guns.

I totaled the number of dead rhinos we had discovered from the beginning and wrote each location in my notebook. My sickening sum ran to twenty-four rhinos killed.

My father's voice at the evening campfire drew me closer to the others. "I know that we are tired and sad. But we must summon our strength and head home at dawn as fast as our elephants can carry us. The rhinos near our stable are better guarded, but they may be the next targets. The poachers fled our area after they killed Pradhan, but now that they have killed many rhinos far from the guard posts, they are emboldened."

I tried to control my growing sense of rage and turn it to something positive, something I knew I could achieve. I would defend our Borderland family with my life. I knew it then. I knew, too, that my elephant brother would do the same.

I needed time to talk to my father and tell him what Hira Prashad and I would dedicate ourselves to do. He rode with me on my tusker back to the stable. He sensed my anger, and kept his one hand on my shoulder as we moved down the trail from

Lalmati to the stable. At first, I thought it was because of the pain from his gout, maybe he needed to keep his balance. But then I realized it was to keep me from exploding.

"*Subba-sahib*, why do men behave like animals? No, that is unfair to animals. Why do they act like demons?"

"Nandu, we will catch them and put a stop to this. Do not worry," he said, squeezing my shoulder.

I could not let it go. "But Kalomutu is in prison and so are the other Maroons who could lead this gang. Do you think Ramji is right, that his evil spirit departs his body or spreads from him to others?"

"Nandu, Kalomutu is not a threat to us. There are others among us, just as ruthless. My Tharu relatives believe the Borderlands are a refuge from evil in the world, protected by Ban Devi. We will make it so again."

I did not believe this was possible anymore. Ban Devi was losing her power over this evil. But I could never say this to my father.

"Ban Devi helped us catch the Maroons last year when they were robbing villages across the Borderlands. I believe she will help us catch these other criminals. And with the help of the police and maybe the army if needed, we will catch them."

"*Subba-sahib*, I think I understand now why these new bandits kill rhinos instead of rob villages like the Maroons," I said.

"Then you must explain it to me," he said.

"Stealing from nature is much easier than robbing people.

If the Maroons steal from poor villagers, hundreds of police officers will scour the jungle for them. If they are caught, they will be sent to jail, just like Kalomutu."

"Yes, that is true."

"But if this new band of outlaws goes after rhinos for their horns, all they have to worry about are men like the warden-*sahib*, who is a coward, and Ganesh Lal, who never speaks, and the guards who spend their days at the *raksi* stalls or who have deserted their posts."

"Yes, Nandu, I felt the same hopelessness, but these people have gone too far. They have killed twenty-four rhinos and stolen their horns. Rhinos are the property of the king. Once Kathmandu hears the news, the palace will mobilize the Royal Nepal Army."

Army soldiers coming to the Borderlands was what we needed. Maybe the king would order a division of fierce Gurkhas to protect the Borderlands. The Gurkhas were known for their fearlessness and skill using the curved blades of their *kukhris*. If a regiment of them came, the poachers would flee for their lives when the Gurkhas drew their blades.

I wanted to say that if the army did not come, Hira Prashad and I would stop the poachers ourselves. Just how, I did not know yet. I needed a plan.

The stable was not far off now. Our elephants knew it, too, and rumbled back and forth. I thought they were rumbling out of happiness to be heading home again, but they were joined by the sound of a small group of sambar deer barking in alarm. From the corner of my eye I saw flashes of red bounding through the grass. It was the *dhole* pack on a hunt. My body relaxed. I turned to say something to my father when a shot rang out.

"*Agat!*" I shouted, but Hira Prashad needed no command. All five elephants turned toward the sound, trumpeting their alarm.

As we grew nearer, I realized we were close to the Baba's temple.

Subba-sahib motioned for the other elephants to fan out, and we did a sweep of the area. No one was about. Not even the Baba. I prayed that he had not been shot by the angry mob. Would they kill a man? A holy man?

Ahead, Dilly let out a sharp whistle and motioned with his arm. We headed toward the ravine near the Baba's temple where the Jogi Khola, the Holy Man's River, flowed. Sprawled in the ravine next to the pool where he used to cool off was the Baba's tiger.

I jumped off Hira Prashad and rolled. I could not wait for him to kneel.

The tiger's front foot had been caught in a wire snare. The

poachers had shot him. It must have only just happened. The Baba's tiger lay motionless.

"We arrived too quickly for them to make off with the tiger," Dilly said. "But too late to catch them, again!"

"*Subba-sahib*, he is still breathing!" I shouted, seeing a faint rise and fall in the fur along the tiger's ribs. "We must save him! Please!"

"We cannot put the tiger on an elephant's back. Even if it is too weak to move, the elephants will not permit us," my father said. "We must fetch Doctor-*sahib* to tranquilize the tiger and remove the bullet here. Dilly, drive Man Kali to get Doctor-*sahib*. Tell the men to have ready one of the empty crates left behind the stable. Tell them to transport the crate to the shed behind the warden's office. After Doctor-*sahib* has treated him we will place the tiger in the crate there."

While we waited, the tiger tried twice to rise but was held back by the snare. The tiger had been shot in the left shoulder and blood trickled down his leg. The snare wound cut deep into his paw. His moans made me shudder in despair.

After thirty minutes that felt like hours, Dilly returned with Doctor-*sahib* clutching his leather medical bag in his lap. The two bounced up and down on the trotting Man Kali.

Quickly, the veterinarian darted the tiger using a blowgun. I had never seen this device before. It looked like a long straw. Soon the tiger was unconscious, and Doctor-*sahib* set to work.

"The dose I gave him should keep him sedated long enough

to remove the bullet and get him to the warden's compound. We must move him quickly, though, once I am finished.

"Nandu, hold this clamp," Doctor-*sahib* ordered. This time I did not flinch or feel sick. "Fortunately, the tiger was moving, or they were bad shots. The bullet missed his heart by six inches."

He pulled out the slug with his forceps and began cleaning the wound. I held the cotton swabs and thought of the Baba. Where was he? Maybe it was better he was not here to see.

In a few minutes the wound was sewn up. We removed the snare and treated the area where the wire had cut the flesh. I helped the drivers tie the tiger's paws together, holding his forelegs. Touching the tiger again reminded me of when Rita and I had put our hands on his beating heart the last time we had helped the Baba's tiger. I moved my hand to his heart again. His pulse was slow.

The oxcart arrived from the stable. We had to release the scared oxen before we loaded the tiger or they would spook by his smell. Ramji herded them back to camp while Dilly and I took their place. I thought this must have been the first time ever a tiger was pulled in an oxcart by two humans.

TWENTY-FOUR

ehind the warden's compound under a tall shed with open sides, I crawled into the crate that would be the tiger's home while he recuperated. A leopard had been in it before. It was roomy for a smaller cat, but it would be a tight fit for the tiger. Before we lifted the Baba's tiger from the cart, I swept the crate clean and wiped the concrete floor with alcohol to sterilize it the best that I could. When the Baba's tiger woke, he would realize that he was trapped again, first by a snare and then pushed into a crate barely longer than he was. He would have to spend at least a week in this prison. I could no longer bear thinking about animals in chains and cages.

We carefully transferred the unconscious tiger into the leopard crate. It took all four of us to lift him, but again Indra's strength saved the day. The tiger remained sedated, but he would wake up soon and probably be very angry.

"You need time to heal before going back into the wild," I whispered to him from outside the crate.

My father described the scene in the Bheri Valley to the warden and Ganesh Lal, who this time immediately headed back inside his office to file his report. With twenty-four more dead rhinos and a tiger wounded probably by the same poachers, he could not keep this from Kathmandu and the king any longer.

I was sitting outside the warden's office under a silk cotton tree when I felt something brush softly against my shoulder. I expected it was a bird, but when I looked it was the Baba. His wrinkled forehead was peaked like a mountain, questioning the fate of his tiger. I stood up and took his hand.

"I will take you to your tiger, Baba," I said. "He is alive."

I led the Baba to the garden, where the tiger's crate sat under the shed. The tiger was still groggy but coming back to consciousness. He gave a low growl that to me sounded like he was unhappy to be confined but happy to see the Baba. My holy friend sank to his knees, closed his eyes, and prayed. I waited until the Baba was finished and had seated himself cross-legged next to the tiger's crate. The Baba counted one, two, three with his fingers, followed by a shrug.

"You are wondering how long the tiger will stay in this cage?" I asked.

The Baba nodded. I was almost as good as Father Autry!

"It will be . . ." The Baba stopped me and pointed to the tiger. Of course, he meant for me to tell the tiger, so he might be less agitated.

"Great King of the Jungle," I addressed the tiger. "You will not be here longer than a week. You must rest while your deep wound heals. You must have medicine so it heals properly and never bothers you again."

I looked at the Baba, who smiled and rested his hand on his heart and then on mine. Last, he held his hand next to the cage, as if to touch the tiger's heart.

"We are family," I said.

The tiger opened his giant mouth in a yawn and relaxed onto his side.

All week the Baba sat there, never leaving the tiger's side. I brought him tea and crackers and that was all he would take. Father Autry bought fresh buffalo meat twice a day from the bazaar for the tiger's meals, which helped him grow stronger by the day. Doctor-*sahib* filled the meat with pills of antibiotics.

"What a powerful constitution this tiger has, Baba," said my father, who had come to visit from the stable. "He will be back hunting deer in a few days. We have searched and removed snares from the forest from here to your temple. There were over a hundred hidden in the undergrowth. I hope our drivers found them all, but I cannot be certain."

The Baba nodded softly and continued chanting his prayers for the tiger's full recovery.

Three days later, Doctor-*sahib* declared that the tiger was strong enough to leave his crate. The Baba's prayers had no doubt speeded his recovery. To return the tiger to the wild, we would have to sedate him again. Doctor-*sahib* used his blow-gun, but with a milder dose. Then Dilly, Indra, and I carried him in the oxcart back to the Baba's temple, with a parade of followers: Father Autry, the Baba, my father, Rita, and Kanchi. Jayanti and Kabita had stayed behind with Maila.

We kept a watchful eye on the sleeping tiger to be sure he came to no harm. Within the hour, he raised his head once, twice, then finally rose to his feet and sauntered off into the jungle.

I walked the Baba back to his temple, before I would catch up with my friends who were heading back on the elephants. The Baba's eyes appeared moist. Then his face relaxed, and his eyes met mine. I tried to read his thoughts.

"Wait," I said. I went into the hut where the Baba slept and retrieved his chalkboard. When I came back I looked into his eyes again. They were softer but still intense.

"You are thanking me for helping to save your tiger a second time."

The Baba nodded.

"But there is more to do. Next time, the tiger may not survive."

The Baba raised his eyebrows and nodded sort of sideways, as if I had interpreted his thoughts in an interesting way. Then he took the chalkboard and drew a picture of his tiger on one side and on the other side some huts meant to be a village. Then he drew a picture of a boy in the middle. Me. Under the drawing he wrote: *Nandu, the bridge.*

I hugged the Baba, repeating the words back to him. I am the bridge. Then a deep inner voice joined the conversation. I do not know if it was Ban Devi or another god or just part of my own self, but I knew in that moment that I must be the protector of all animals. I must act and not count on anyone else.

I stood barefoot next to Hira Prashad feeding him his *kuchis* by hand. The cool earth against my soles was calming. This way, too, I could feel the vibrations of the elephants' deepest sounds, as they stood receiving their *kuchis* at the end of a long workday. I did not want to chain my elephants at night anymore. I had to come up with a solution that would keep them safe but also let them have their dignity. I was the bridge, as the Baba had told me. I would find a way.

My tusker seemed at peace, though, even with all the activity swirling round us. He focused on his treats, and if I hesitated, he banged his trunk against the ground for more. He had eaten half of his twenty-five *kuchis* in just a few minutes.

"Number thirteen, Hira Prashad." I reached out to hand it to him. But instead of taking it from me, he spread his ears wide and lifted his trunk. No sound came out, but I was sure I felt the air move around us. Hira Prashad left the *kuchi* in my hand and started off down the trail into the jungle. He had never done that before. It was like he had read my mind about wanting him to be free.

"Dilly, Hira Prashad is running off!" I yelled. "Follow me on Man Kali, and bring some ropes. And tell *Subba-sahib*. Hira Prashad senses trouble!"

I ran down the familiar trail, and before long I could see Hira Prashad's back. I had to keep running to keep him in view. I chased after him for a long time until I was out of breath. Finally, he slowed enough that I could catch up and speak to him.

"Hira Prashad, please stop. It is too dangerous to be walking alone in this jungle. It is too dangerous for me, too. At least let me ride on your back."

I could see the elephants from the stable hustling up the trail by the dust they had stirred up. They would be here in several minutes.

Instead of waiting, Hira Prashad took off again heading straight for the Lalmati grassland.

"Raaa!" I shouted, but he ignored my command. I wanted to follow him, but I waited for my father and Dilly. Other drivers had come, too. I climbed aboard Jun Kali, our fastest elephant. We moved so quickly as if the forest was flying by on either side of us.

Our five elephants finally reached the lower end of Lalmati. In the center of the grassland, Hira Prashad stood with his back toward us. Next to him was the herd of wild elephants. They had formed a tight circle. It was too dangerous to approach on foot. We waited for the herd to break apart so we could see what drew Hira Prashad to their side.

"*Subba-sahib*, maybe Hira Prashad's rival has moved away from the Great Sand Bar River," I whispered.

My father simply stared ahead. He was not my father now but the shaman. I had lost him to his murmuring trance. The sun was setting, and the trees in the distance were turning into a dark scalloped silhouette.

A black cutout veered through the sky. A vulture swooped low into a tree followed by another and another.

My father gave a hand signal for the other elephants to stay back. On my father's command, he and I and the driver of Jun Kali would approach the herd. We moved cautiously at first, but soon we realized the herd was not interested in us. The wild females next to Hira Prashad were in mourning.

I stood up on Jun Kali to look over the circle of elephants. In the middle was the body of a large elephant I did not recognize. I could only see the hind end. One of them had passed. The elephants were in mourning, I was sure of it. Hira Prashad stepped to the side to let us in. I thought of my Devi Kali. Maybe it was an old female gone to join her.

But it was not an old female. In the center of the circle was

Hira Prashad's rival. The great wild tusker. His beautiful ivory tusks were gone. Hacked off his face with an ax. I had never seen anything as gruesome.

We quickly retreated and my father relayed the horrible news. I hung my head. This nightmare would not end. I worried it never would. I could not bridge this divide between the human and the wild. No one could.

"We must head back to the stable," my father said.

"But Hira Prashad. We cannot leave him here," I said.

"It is too dangerous for you to try to mount him now. We have to hope that he returns on his own. I cannot help him either. He is between worlds."

My eyes filled with tears. I could not leave my brother out here to be slaughtered, but he had a right to be an elephant. To think like an elephant. To live like an elephant. I could not stand in his way. I could not make him safe only for my sake.

PART V

UPRISING

TWENTY-FIVE

I had listened for Hira Prashad far into the night, but all I heard was the empty *chunk-chunk-chunk* of the nightjars and the hooting of a forest owl. A leopard passed by camp and made its sawing-wood sound. I knew it was hopeless, I would be up all night.

By morning, by some miracle, Hira Prashad had returned. Even though he was not chained to his tethering post, he stood next to it, calmly as ever.

I ran to him. My tusker bowed his head, and I climbed up over his head by grabbing the tips of his ears in my hands and stepping on his trunk while he lifted me over his head, just as I had with his mother, our mother, Devi Kali, when I was a boy. I lay down on the length of his back and let myself cry all the tears I'd held back: for the rhinos, for the tiger, for the great wild tusker. Hira Prashad raised his trunk over his head and snorted, smelling my tears. The air from his breathing ruffled my hair. "Thank you, brother," I said, patting his great head.

Across the worn grass, on the other side of my father's gazebo, Rita and her crew had finished feeding their charges. Kabita, Jayanti, and Kanchi were brushing the little jumbos. Maila was scratching the baby rhinos under their chins while they waited their turn with the brush. He would get his cast removed today and run like a healthy boy again. There were a few happy things to look forward to in this bleak time.

I decided that day, after Indra and I had grazed Hira Prashad, that I would visit Father Autry to break the news about the wild tusker and seek his advice about how to protect Hira Prashad. When I reached my tutor's bungalow, he came out to meet me, as if he knew I was coming.

"Nandu, I have already heard the sad news. Let us go visit the Baba."

Along the way to the temple, I asked him, "Father-*sahib*, who is behind all this? How can men be so cruel?"

"These are awful men, Nandu, who kill these magnificent animals for no good reason. Only for money. But there are forces behind them, those who never get their hands dirty, who put the poachers up to this. We must find out who they are and expose them."

There was nothing else to say. My tutor and I walked in silence until we reached the Baba's temple. We quietly joined the Baba by his morning fire. The flames were dying, but no one added any kindling. The smoke swirled around and stung our eyes, making us wince.

I spoke up first. "Baba, are wild animals on earth just for us to abuse them?"

The Baba did not answer me. Instead he looked deep into my eyes and touched his fingers into a pouch he had tied to his waist. A colored powder came out this time. He touched the warm ash to my head, rose, and walked into his temple to pray.

I know the Baba did not think of these ashes as war paint, but that is how they seemed to me. This was war. A war to save our wildlife and our jungle. And I was ready to fight to the end.

⸺

After I grazed the elephants, Maila greeted me and motioned with his bow and arrow. I think he wanted me to go hunting with him, but I was too busy and needed to talk to my father. I did not know how to tell him I did not hunt. I motioned that I had work to do. Maila seemed to understand and headed off toward the river.

He did not return that day or evening. I got up several times in the night to look out the window for him. There was no Maila. I woke with the crowing of the red jungle fowl and I looked over at Maila's cot. He was not there.

I found him waiting for me outside the cookhouse, smiling. Next to him was a large burlap bag with something inside it. He reached up and put his hand to my heart and mine to his. He opened the sack and dragged out what was folded up inside. It was a langur monkey, with an arrow piercing its chest.

Maila looked up at me and grinned with delight. His face changed instantly when I screamed. "No!"

Maila ran off as fast as he could, leaving me alone with the dead langur. I was so angry I could not see how badly I had scared him. I did not care. Poachers were killing our wildlife left and right. I knew Maila meant well, but his gift was a shock.

I spent the rest of the day looking for him with Kanchi's help.

"Kanchi, Maila did not understand why I screamed. I am sure he feels crushed."

"Do not feel bad, Nandu. He was about to leave us anyway. He told me he was going, but he said to keep it a secret. He pointed to himself and then made a sign with his fingers, like walking away. Then he held his finger to his lips."

"I feel so awful for shouting at him. I see he meant well."

Kanchi grabbed my hand and said, "Nandu, he has gone off to find his own again. You gave him that chance and he was thankful. For his people, to give food, the monkey, is the greatest gift."

By evening it was clear that he had slipped away, back into the hills.

It seemed everyone was disappearing. Hira Prashad slipped his chain (which I had loosened) that night, too, and was off into the jungle again. He was probably checking on the wild herd. But I worried about the poachers spotting him.

"He is part of two herds now," my father said. "This makes it even harder to keep an eye on him. We may have to organize another search party."

We were expecting a visit from the conservator-*sahib* that afternoon. If Hira Prashad was not here, it would be hard to explain his absence. My father would be held accountable. An hour later, there was still no sign of our tusker. We were about to head out on the elephants, when Dilly whistled sharply. I knew what that meant. Down the track to our stable, the conservator-*sahib*'s car made a cloud of dust. Four other passengers rode with him.

When the car pulled into camp, it stopped abruptly. We saw now that the Mr. Rijal had brought Doctor-*sahib*, who held the door open for an army general. Dhungel-*sahib* came next, and last, Ganesh Lal. News of all the poaching must have reached Kathmandu.

We formally bowed to the army general, who nodded to my father.

"*Subba-sahib*, the twenty-four rhinos were bad enough. But now the warden tells me that a giant tusker has also been killed," the conservator-*sahib* said. "What are we going to do, *Subba-sahib*? Must His Majesty call in the army?"

Before *Subba-sahib* could respond, shouts from the far end of the stable interrupted him. Coming up the path from the jungle was Hira Prashad. Following behind him was the dead bull's wild herd. The officials, except for the army general and Ganesh Lal, jumped back into their jeep as soon as they saw them. The elephants moved slowly, like they were guiding a newborn. Hira Prashad was heading straight for where we stood with Doctor-*sahib*.

When he was twenty feet from us, Hira Prashad turned around and walked into the circle of females. They parted and we saw for the first time the elephant in their midst. Limping badly, surrounded by the adults, was not a newborn calf but what looked to be a ten-year-old female. Her right front foot had been caught in a poacher's wire snare, part of which was now embedded and swollen around it.

"Doctor-*sahib*," my father said, "I think that Hira Prashad recognizes you and trusts you to heal this elephant like you did for the Baba's tiger. He has brought her to you."

"*Subba-sahib*, to treat this young female and remove the snare, I will have to get next to it to inject a tranquilizer. I cannot fire a tranquilizer through the blowgun like I did for the tiger. Elephant skin is too tough. I worry that if I raise my darting rifle, the elephants might panic. They could charge us or flee."

Seeing there was no immediate danger, the conservator-*sahib* came out of the vehicle to talk with us, but the warden wanted no part. He stayed in the jeep. Our drivers and the officials stood around, debating what to do next.

Kanchi did not wait for them. She grabbed some *kuchis* meant for the little jumbos and walked straight up to the suffering elephant. She fed the injured female from her hand. Hira Prashad stood next to her and rumbled to the others. Kanchi started to stroke the young female's trunk. Then she stood on her tiptoes and whispered something into its ear.

"Doctor-*sahib*, I think it is now safe to inject the tranquilizer and treat the wound. Come, Nandu and I will help you," my father said.

The wild herd stood by and watched from a distance. It occurred to me that in this moment we were all on a magical bridge between worlds. For this brief time, there was no wild and no human, only healing and help from family.

Doctor-*sahib* gave the young female a quick injection and in minutes she was on her side. Rita and Indra carried buckets of hot water. After Doctor-*sahib* removed the wire snare, Kanchi held it up for the elephants to see and tossed it in front of them so they could smell it. Then she went back to helping Doctor-*sahib* clean the wound.

"At least this is one elephant we can save," said Doctor-*sahib*.

Hira Prashad and the older females gathered around the snare and touched it with their trunks, like they were trying to smell the person who had set it. I held the elephant's ear while Doctor-*sahib* gave his patient the antidote to the sedative in a large vein. She clambered back to her feet in thirty seconds.

Hira Prashad rumbled deeply, offering thanks to Doctor-*sahib* and Kanchi, and the wild herd and our stable elephants echoed their thanks, too. I knew it could not last. But for a moment we were one herd.

TWENTY-SIX

K anchi had more time on her hands since Maila had left. Her thoughts drifted to becoming a *mahout*. I told her she would be great. I did not tell her it would be a battle with my father, not to mention the other drivers.

She watched Indra and me climb on Hira Prashad. I knew she would want to join us. "Where are you going, Nandu?" she called.

Indra looked at me. We had made a pact not to tell anybody.

"*Subba-sahib* told us that the king has dispatched an army platoon of Gurkhas to catch the poachers," I told her. "Indra and I are going to the ridge to see if we can see them coming."

This was a bit of a lie. I could not wait for an army to come. Every day that our animals had no protection was a day more could die. I had persuaded Indra to come with me. It did not take many words. We were going after the poachers before they could strike again.

"I am coming with you," she said, giving orders, just like *Subba-sahib*.

"Kanchi, you are needed here," I said. "Besides, it is not safe now. There are thugs in the jungle, waiting to attack."

"I am not afraid. I want to help protect our elephants and the rhinos, the families of Rona and Ritu and the little jumbos. They are my family, too!" Kanchi shouted.

Indra rolled his eyes. I shook my head.

"I am coming, and if you do not let me on Hira Prashad, I will follow you on foot," Kanchi added.

Even though Indra and I were not persuaded, my elephant was. He took two steps backward and dropped to his knees to let Kanchi climb up. There is no arguing with an elephant, especially my tusker.

When Kanchi was comfortably situated behind me in the saddle, she said, "Thank you, Hira Prashad."

"So you can talk to elephants now," I said, joking, but also slightly jealous, since it did appear to be the case.

I drove Hira Prashad to our favorite spot, the ridge where he had saved my life during the earthquake. This way Kanchi would think that we were looking northeast to Kathmandu, but I was really scanning the river below for signs of a camp. The poachers were hiding somewhere in our jungle. I was certain they were still here, somewhere near water.

Soon we were trotting along on a path bordered by

blooming wild butterfly bush. The perfume covered us in its sweet fragrance.

"Indra, do you remember the story that Father Autry told us when we went to the Bheri River Valley? The one about Hannibal, who crossed the high mountains on his war elephants? His tuskers surprised and scared the Romans, and they surrendered. Too bad we cannot train these Gurkhas to ride elephants. It would be such a fitting victory for the poachers to be defeated by the very animals they killed."

When we reached the top of the ridge, Indra and I stood atop Hira Prashad. I took up my binoculars and scanned the horizon in the direction of Kathmandu.

"That is a silly idea, Nandu. You will not see the army marching from Kathmandu. It is too hilly. You cannot even see the road." Kanchi was another smart one.

"I thought we might see a sign. Some dust from afar."

Kanchi eyed me suspiciously. "I think you want to protect the animals yourself. And we should!"

Kanchi turned herself around and looked out over the landscape to the south. I sat down next to her. "You are right. We cannot sit by and wait for the army. If one more animal dies, and I could have saved it . . ."

"You do not need to explain it to me," Kanchi said. "Nandu, I have to tell you a secret that Maila told me. He told me not to tell anyone."

"Is it about the poachers?"

"Maybe. He said that when he was out hunting, he saw two men camped near Clear Lake. They saw him and he ran and hid. He is so good at hiding. He waited until night to return to camp."

"Was this the night he brought me the monkey?"

Kanchi nodded.

"They could still be there!"

Indra and I looked at one another. Hira Prashad had been right to bring Kanchi along. We headed down from the ridge toward the trail to Clear Lake. The lake was still two hours away, but we rode in silence. Elephants can move like ghosts when they want to. Maybe Hira Prashad wanted revenge, too. If he charged the poachers, I already made up my mind that I would not stop him.

When we reached the southern edge of Clear Lake, no one was about.

"Kanchi," I whispered. "This is the exact spot where *Subba-sahib* and Devi Kali found me, when I was guarded by the *dhole*."

I had no sooner said the words than I saw my pack. The leader, skinny with a slightly hunched back, looked at us once, then started to run along a different trail. The pack came to a sudden stop and they all looked back at us again, as if they were asking for us to follow.

"Kanchi," I whispered. "You wait here on Hira Prashad.

Indra and I will come back as soon as we see what is ahead. Do *not* climb down."

Indra and I followed the *dhole* on foot. When they raised their tails we dropped down on all fours to scout up ahead. I smelled the smoke of a campfire. We were downwind of whoever was tending it. They probably kept it smoky to keep the horseflies at bay. Two landed on my arm, but I dared not slap at them.

We crawled closer and looked through the leaves of the wild coffee bushes. Crouched in front of the fire was the one-eyed Maroon. He had not drowned when Hira Prashad chased him into the Great Sand Bar River. This rat had crawled out of the water. Eight other men were standing around a buckboard wagon attached to a pair of oxen. Three of them I recognized. There was the village headman that confronted us at the Khatta jungle and the other who had wanted to spear the Baba's tiger. The third was part of the same village mob. They were the ones who were likely feeding the poachers information about the locations of the rhinos, and about the movements of our stable. Somehow, I half expected Ganesh Lal to be among them or the guards from the Chisapani and Bheri posts, but they were not there. Nor was the man from the Bichia bazaar, selling the ivory trinkets.

The biggest surprise though was when the man driving the wagon turned around. He was the one who had stared at Hira

Prashad that day that he and the boy were fishing by the Great Sand Bar River. Now I knew that man was not the boy's father. Like Kanchi, his parents had probably taken money in return for the boy's help. They were not fishing that day. They were spying on us and the wildlife.

I was shaking from the suddenness of these discoveries. Then I regained my senses and focused on our mission. I whispered to Indra, "Here is the whole gang."

He nodded. "Nandu, we should go back and make sure that Kanchi is still sitting on Hira Prashad and not preparing to drive him into their camp. She would do it!"

The poachers kept a rack of guns propped between two trees. We could not drive Hira Prashad into their camp. It was too dangerous. We would need more help. I nodded to Indra, and we crawled back.

Kanchi had followed my request, surprisingly enough, and was still sitting on Hira Prashad, swatting at the horseflies trying to bite both her and my elephant with a branch she had cut on her own.

"Kanchi, we have found them. But they have many guns. You and Indra must drive Hira Prashad back to the stable. I can track them better alone. You must alert *Subba-sahib* and have him bring the men from the stable to Clear Lake. We will meet you back here."

"Nandu, we should stay together," Kanchi said.

"No, I am going to follow the two on the wagon to see

where they take it. They may still have the ivory and rhino horns in it." I thought of what Father Autry said about tracking the poachers back to their ringleaders.

Kanchi did not want to leave. I looked pleadingly at Indra. "I will go, Nandu. Kanchi, you come with me. We will meet Nandu here with all the drivers and elephants and the police." He tapped Hira Prashad on the shoulder, but the great tusker would not leave my side.

I whispered in Hira Prashad's giant ear and shared my new idea. "We will catch these men, Hira Prashad. Please take Kanchi back to the stable and go get *Subba-sahib* and the other elephants." No more commands were needed. My tusker turned and headed back to the stable.

I ran down the trail that paralleled the most direct track through the forest—the one that the driver of the wagon would take. I ran for five minutes as fast as I could, until I saw the wagon again. I slowed to a walk, but stayed close enough to keep it in view. I could see the driver, the bearded man, and sitting next to him was the village headman who had confronted the Baba. He had a rifle in his lap and another on a sling over his shoulder. There must have been something valuable under the tarp covering the wagon.

I followed the wagon out of the jungle for the next two hours. The driver turned right at a fork in the forest trail, then headed toward Gobrechar, the village that is the home of the local landlord, the one we call the Python. This was the demon who nearly killed Hira Prashad for his ivory before Dilly and I rescued him.

The wagon took another turn down a dirt road, and before I knew it we were back where my contact with Hira Prashad first began—at the large house and courtyard belonging to the Python. The village headman got out and opened the gate to the courtyard to let the wagon roll in.

How strange to be back here, looking into this wretched courtyard, and yet, it made perfect sense that the Python was behind the poachers. I peeked over the wall. And when I was sure no one was watching, I carefully approached the window to see inside.

Sitting in a large chair across from the Python was Dhungel-*sahib*, the warden.

My anger shot up like a geyser, but I knew I had to stay quiet and stick with our plan. We would catch the warden later and he could join the Python and the Maroons in prison.

I approached the wagon. Barely lifting the canvas, I saw their crimes: Inside were the tusks of the giant male elephant and the horns of twenty-four rhinos. I thought about how many animals had died, enough rhinos to start a population in a new reserve. Now their giant bodies were reduced to two dozen horns and a pair of tusks.

A hand lightly tapped my shoulder.

I spun around to find Kanchi. She had been following me the whole time.

I motioned for her to sneak back out of the courtyard. Even outside the walls, we had to stay quiet, so I could not express my fury at her. We heard the wagon moving again. It rolled out the gate and left the Python's residence. We had to keep going.

The wailing of the peacocks covered up the noise of the squeaking of the wagon frame as it moved through the narrow jungle track. We walked all afternoon in the cool late-day breeze with the dried leaves fluttering down from the trees. It was mid-November and the temperature would drop at dusk to just above freezing. Neither Kanchi nor I had on warm clothes. But we had to keep moving to see where these poachers were going. I was following Father Autry's advice to find the men on the other side of the deal.

We walked quickly but always keeping a safe distance. The wagon would speed up and then slow down, speed up and slow down, making us tense and exhausted. The long day had pushed us beyond what I thought either of us could endure.

When we reached the edge of the forest, before the vegetable fields bordering the town, the bearded Maroon stopped for a break. Thankfully, we could take a short rest, too. We ducked behind the trunk of an old acacia tree, now full of egrets about to roost for the night. A squirt of fresh bird droppings landed on Kanchi's back. I wiped it off quickly, brushing my arm over her, like I was guiding her to crouch lower. I said nothing. But in the Borderlands, we believe having a bird's droppings land on you brings bad luck. We did not need any more; we had plenty enough.

I did not know what to do with Kanchi. I could not send her back alone, nor could I let the wagon out of my sight. We simply had to keep moving.

By the time we reached Gularia, it was almost dark. The wagon stopped at a boardinghouse outside town.

The two poachers got down from the wagon and grabbed their rifles, standing guard, waiting. From across the street, we could make out another man coming out of the building. He walked over to the poachers and lifted the canvas covering the buckboard.

The man looked pleased. He signaled for two more men to come over. They quickly loaded the ivory and horns from the wagon into a jeep. When they were done, the jeep motor turned on, but the men did not leave. Finally, a third man stepped out of the house. I squinted in the fading light. He looked familiar. When the jeep's headlights illuminated his face, I recognized Ganesh Lal instantly.

Ganesh Lal handed the poachers a large envelope, then jumped into the jeep.

"Kanchi, I was right. Ganesh Lal is a part of this." Before I could say more, the jeep roared off, with Ganesh Lal in it, leaving behind the poachers and the now-empty wagon. We had been too late. The horns and ivory were on their way, destined to the carvers and medicine stalls. My heart felt so heavy. Kanchi squeezed my arm. She could sense my dismay. Maybe we could at least catch this gang and they could report that traitor Ganesh Lal. How ironic, I thought, that his name was Ganesh, after the elephant god. What dishonor he brought to it.

Under a bare bulb hung outside the house, we watched the man with the beard—the fake fisherman—counting his money. It took some time. He said something to the village headman and they both laughed. The poachers climbed back into the seats of the buckboard wagon and headed off the way we had come. "Nandu, they are all leaving," said Kanchi. "We must notify the police."

"Kanchi, I am going to follow the empty wagon. You go hide at the edge of town in the jungle by that old acacia tree. Wait there until I come for you. Take a rest and put my shirt over you to stay warm. Do not go to the police." I remembered my last time going to the Gularia police station, and I did not want Kanchi to have to spend a night in jail as I had.

I waited until the wagon was one hundred yards up the track before I started following. A half mile later, I had a sense that Kanchi was not far behind. I had no choice now but to let her stay with me.

TWENTY-SEVEN

The wagon continued rolling along the dirt track out of Gularia carrying two rich men who had made our jungle much poorer by their crimes. After we turned once, I thought we were headed back to Clear Lake, but I could not be sure.

Indra must have made it back to the stable, I thought. By now the police would be on the way. It would be too dangerous for our elephants to confront so many armed poachers without the police.

Kanchi and I kept up a steady whisper. The turning wheels and the bouncing of the buckboard on the rough track made enough noise to cover up our voices. "Kanchi, I think they are heading back to their camp. We will hide in the boulders above Clear Lake and wait until the men from our stable and the police arrive."

"Nandu, we must stay awake the whole time."

We kept alert until we were about an hour away from Clear Lake. Kanchi's legs gave out and she became too tired to walk. I put her on my back and carried her, but our pace slowed. Finally, we reached the edge of the poachers' camp and the wagon stopped. The men were talking and jumped off the buckboard. The others greeted them with bottles of liquor.

"Kanchi, they will drink all night and fall asleep. Maybe we can steal their guns." But Kanchi had already fallen asleep on my back. We moved behind some bushes and crouched out of view. Within seconds my eyes shut, too.

We woke to the bright morning sun in our eyes. Standing above us was the bearded Maroon. In his hand was a long knife. Kanchi tried to run, but the men grabbed her by her long braid. They tied our hands and legs and we were hauled into the camp. Kanchi squeezed my wrist and held on tight.

Our only hope now was that *Subba-sahib* would arrive soon with the police. I was so angry that I had allowed Kanchi to follow the wagon with me. I had put her in such danger.

An hour later, we were hunched down with our backs to each other, a tree sapling between us. They bound us with another set of ropes, hand and foot. I sat facing the men while Kanchi looked out at the rocky hillside above the camp. I was glad she had a less scary view and perhaps could not overhear the men, who sat around their campfire, debating what to do with us. There was no sign of the boy who I had caught setting snares. Perhaps they had sent him back to India, back to his family.

Eye Patch spoke first. His gravelly voice spooked me.

"I want to strangle that one first," he said, pointing at me. "He is dead for taking my eye out a year ago. Then he stole that girl and two others from me."

The long-bearded man, the fake fisherman who was clearly the leader of the poachers in this gang, the one who had driven the wagon, said nothing.

"Then I will strangle her. She got away twice from me. Not a third time."

The other six men stared into the fire. I think they were afraid of Eye Patch. I squeezed Kanchi's fingers.

Eye Patch stood up and started toward us. I prepared to lunge at him with my feet and kick him in the head when he got close.

"Wait, brother," said the long-bearded Maroon. "I have a better plan. We can use these two."

Eye Patch turned around.

"Here is what we will do. We will send the master of the elephant stable a letter written by this boy. We will offer an exchange. The boy for that tusker's ivory. They give us the ivory, we release the girl. The boy crosses the Indian border with us. Once we sell the ivory, we release the boy. Then we head home with enough money for each of us to buy a palace in Bihar."

"What if they are already on the way?" asked the headman who had confronted the Baba and accompanied Long Beard to Gularia. The other men nodded. "Better to leave now. We have all the money we need from the rhinos and tusker. Let us divide the money and leave these two here."

Long Beard whipped out his pistol. "Anyone who leaves now will be hunted and shot."

The headman raised his hands in submission.

"Those of you who stay will earn an extra ten thousand rupees each when we get the ivory from that tusker. Now, we must move north of the lake. From there we can see anyone approaching."

The men nodded and raised their drinks. They made a toast to Long Beard.

"That tusker nearly trampled me," Eye Patch said. "I will be happy to see him gone." He raised his mug to me and then spat on the ground. When they had enough drink, the men took us to the new camp. I hoped our scent was strong enough for Hira Prashad to track us.

The wailing of peacocks and whinnying sound of woodpeckers in the trees above me woke me from sleep. One of the poachers untied all but one leg and handed us mugs of tea and some stale biscuits. Then he told us we could pee where we were sitting. Behind me, I could hear Kanchi sniff to keep from crying.

Long Beard walked up to me holding a lined notebook and a pen. He untied my hands.

"You will write to your *Subba-sahib*," he said. Then he started dictating the letter. When he got to the part about my father poisoning Hira Prashad for his tusks, it was too much.

"I will not write this," I said.

"Then we will cut off your friend's nose, and then an ear," snarled Eye Patch.

I wrote him a note that I knew my father would not be able to read. Maybe he would ask Father Autry to read it, too. I did not think these Maroons could understand Devanagari script, so I wrote, *Please bring something to treat insect bites. The horseflies here are thick*, in small print. My father and the other elephant drivers knew that the worst place for horseflies in the jungle was at the base of the hills next to Clear Lake. A horsefly landed on my bound arm and bit hard. I had never been so thankful for them. If this worked, I would tell *Subba-sahib* we must do a special *puja* to offer thanks to horseflies.

Long Beard grabbed the notebook, and looked over my handwriting. He appeared to be reading the note several times. The more he pondered the more I realized he probably could not read twenty words. My gamble had worked.

Long Beard tied my hands back together. I twisted around to make eye contact with Kanchi before he lashed my back to the tree. I had only had a glimpse of the hillside before I was thrust down on the ground, but I saw a flash of red in the dense bushes. My *dhole*.

Long Beard sent two of the village poachers to walk to Thakurdwara. They were to steal into our stable in the middle of the night and leave the message tacked to my father's bungalow door. It would take them about three hours fast-walking each way.

While they discussed their horrible plan, I took a closer look at the line of rifles and guns. There were six that looked like army rifles, and two shotguns. I hoped that the police would arrive well armed or with a platoon of Gurkhas. Against the tree were coils and coils of wire snares. There must have been hundreds of them. And next to the pile of pistols were three axes covered in dried blood. I did not want to think of how the blood got there. But I knew.

The afternoon wore on and the birds quieted down.

"What do we do if they do not come?" asked Eye Patch.

"They will come for these two. You can count on that. It may take them a day or two after they poison the elephant for it to die."

The sun was sinking through the *sal* forests. I was facing east and I could not see it. Maybe I had seen my last sunset in this life. I thought about how much I loved my father and Hira Prashad. I prayed to Ban Devi, and then to Lord Buddha, and even to Father Autry's God, to any god listening now: *Please let my father know how much I loved him. Save Hira Prashad.*

And please save Kanchi and me.

TWENTY-EIGHT

The rising sun warmed us, as its rays filtered through the forest around Clear Lake. The poachers had thrown a thin blanket over Kanchi and me. It was not thick enough to keep us from shivering through the cool night. Kanchi and I pressed our backs against each other where they touched at the side of the sapling.

Trying to stay warm all night and exhaustion kept me from thinking about the decision facing my father when he found my letter tacked to the door of his bungalow. The two poachers sent to deliver the note had still not returned. Maybe our drivers had spotted their shadows moving across the stable to reach my father's bungalow and captured them? Maybe Hira Prashad heard their footsteps, slipped his chains, and crushed them like one of Hannibal's elephants would.

I could not bear to think of the look on my father's face. How angry he must have been at me and Indra for going off like this and taking Kanchi with us. Several times in the night I woke to hear her softly half crying, half singing a song she made up about a young girl from Jumla who is lost in the mountains and rescued by an elephant.

There was a scrambling sound on the rocky hilltop above us. I heard a *dhole* whistle and whine as loud as if he was next to me. The rest of the pack picked up the call and joined in. The whistling and yowling seemed to echo off the green wall of forest around Clear Lake, waking the few poachers who were still in their sleeping bags.

"Damn dogs!" shouted Eye Patch. I watched the one-eyed Maroon pick up his rifle and aim it at the rocky hills behind me. I heard two shots and panicked. Kanchi grabbed my hand.

———

I could not see it, but I sensed the air moving in waves around us. I knew this feeling from standing next to our elephants. Right then, behind me, I heard Hira Prashad's familiar rumble, answered by the rumble of what sounded like an army—of elephants.

The Maroons were surrounded by a circle of elephants. Some had drivers sitting on them, our men, but others had none. It was the wild herd. They had mixed with our elephants to rescue us. The poachers from the village fell on their knees. Long Beard raced over to me with Eye Patch. The bearded Maroon and his one-eyed henchman cut Kanchi and me loose from the tree.

My father got off his elephant with Dilly. In Dilly's hand was my father's old shotgun.

"You will give us safe passage out of here if you want these captives returned to you alive," yelled Long Beard.

My legs were free but numb from sitting so long. Long Beard gripped his hand across my chest, holding me like a shield. Eye Patch grabbed Kanchi and held her in front of him.

I heard whistles from the rocks behind and above us. The *chir* pheasants had been frightened, too, and were calling in alarm. But then more whistles cut through the air. These were different sounds. Suddenly, Long Beard released his hold and dropped to the ground in front of me. He grabbed his right shoulder. A large arrow was lodged deep into his arm.

Next Eye Patch slumped to the ground in front of Kanchi, with arrows stuck in his neck and shoulders.

I grabbed Kanchi and held her close. Standing above the rocks was Maila, surrounded by the Raute.

I pointed. "Look!"

Maila waved to us, then disappeared with his family behind the boulders. Kanchi was scrambling up the rocks, trying to get one last look at her friend.

"Kanchi, come back!"

At the top of the boulders, she stopped. The Raute had slipped back into the jungle. She stayed there for some time, hoping Maila would return.

Our drivers bound the arms of the poachers with ropes they had brought along.

"Throw them into the wagon," my father said. "The army general will be waiting at the warden's office."

———

On our trip home, the air vibrated victoriously from the crush of elephants around us. The wild herd shadowed our journey, and now that we had arrived at camp, they hovered at the edge of the forest, rumbling back and forth.

Kabita, Jayanti, and Rita ran to greet us, their little jumbos prancing along with them, squealing in delight.

"Kanchi! Nandu!" they yelled in relief.

The girls hugged one another and then me and then the elephants. There were arms and ears and trunks everywhere.

Father Autry and the Baba stopped by to greet us. Instead of shaking my hand, Father Autry did something he had never done before. He grabbed me in his arms and picked me up in a bear hug. And then he did the same to Kanchi. He did not say anything but pulled out his handkerchief to wipe his eyes.

Happiness pulsed through me. Hira Prashad was unharmed, the poachers were in custody of the police, and Kanchi was safe. And Maila had not left us. He had saved us.

TWENTY-NINE

The brotherhood I felt between Dilly and me, or Indra and me, is special, but I never chained them to a tethering pole. I decided I would no longer chain my tusker, either. He had saved me once again and now Kanchi. I stroked his trunk and fed him extra *kuchis* I had made that morning. There was nothing much more to do. The army had come and arrested Mr. Dhungel, the warden, and taken him back to Kathmandu in chains, along with the Python, Long Beard, Eye Patch, and hill tribesmen who had threatened the Baba's tiger. I was not there to watch, but as I looked at the empty crate behind the warden's office, I wished these men could have been thrown in Baba's tiger's pen to be transported back. They deserved no less.

My father and I walked over to the office, where the conservator-*sahib* was waiting for us.

To our surprise, sitting behind the warden's desk was Ganesh Lal. "*Subba-sahib*, Ganesh Lal has agreed to stay on as a

temporary replacement until the palace sends us a new warden," said Mr. Rijal proudly.

"But I saw you! I saw you at the house in Gularia where the
poachers delivered the rhino horns and the ivory," I said.

"Nandu, you saw an undercover agent crack the worst
gang of smugglers in all of Nepal," said the conservator-*sahib*.
"We call him Ganesh Lal, but that is not his real name. The palace sent him to us once our intelligence service learned about
a poaching gang that included two of the old Maroons and
the Python. We transferred the warden here on purpose. He
was being watched, too. We could not tell either of you about
Ganesh-*sahib*'s mission."

"I am sorry I could not share my secret. And I am sorry we
could not prevent more of the poaching. You lost these wonderful animals. It will not happen again," said Ganesh Lal.

That was only the second time I had ever heard him speak.
My mouth hung wide open, and then I did something I never
thought I would do. I bowed to Ganesh Lal or whatever his
name was. My father, who never bows to anybody but the king
and queen, did the same.

My gaze wandered over to the wall where the photos hung
of the now disgraced Dhungel-*sahib* bowing before the king to
receive his medal. He had been arrested so quickly, before he
could flee, that no one had yet taken them down.

Mr. Rijal noticed me staring and laughed. I liked him

again. His incompetence was all a ruse to trick Dhungel the dung beetle into thinking no one was watching. The same for Ganesh Lal.

"You see, Nandu," said the conservator-*sahib*, "this quiet gentleman, Mr. Ganesh Lal, led us in his jeep with the stolen horns all the way to Kathmandu, to the home of the ringleader in Nepal, the godfather of all poaching, and he is behind bars, too."

"Nandu, I could not have brought these criminals to justice if it was not for the courage shown by you and Kanchi. Where is she? I want to thank her, too," said Ganesh, the part-time game scout.

I raced back from the warden's office to find her. I found Rita and Jayanti feeding the Ancient Babies and Nani. Kanchi had stayed back in the girls' room next to the cookhouse. The girls thought she had caught a cold during the two nights we spent tied up to the tree, so I decided to let her rest. She could meet Ganesh Lal another time.

By the afternoon, Rita came by where Dilly, Indra, and I were making *kuchis*. "I think there is something wrong with Kanchi."

"What do you mean?" I said.

"She cannot get out of bed except to vomit and go to the bathroom. She has a fever and a headache. *Subba-sahib* just went over to look at her."

We dropped the *kuchis* and rushed over. When I passed the elephants they were all standing still. They had turned toward the cookhouse with their ears spread wide.

"Nandu, Dilly, Indra, carry Kanchi on this cot to my bungalow. I will treat her there," said my father. Kanchi's face looked drawn and pale. Kabita and Jayanti held on to each other.

"I am going to get Father Autry," I said.

My father nodded. I think he knew that we might need something stronger for her than the plant remedies he could fix.

I ran to my tutor's bungalow and banged on the door. Within minutes, we were in his car with his driver and rolling back into camp.

"Good day, *Subba-sahib*. Please come outside and let us talk."

I stood with them and listened. "What are her symptoms?"

"Father-*sahib*, at first she had headaches and then stomachaches, and now she is too warm and has a rash. I fear that she has the fever."

"*Subba-sahib*, this sounds like typhoid. If so, there is no time to lose. We must get fluids into her."

"*Subba-sahib*, I think we need to go to Bichia and fetch Dr. Aziz. He will know what to do," I said.

My father nodded, like he knew as shaman what he could do and what he could not. "If you can bring back pomegranates, lots of them, I can at least feed her the seeds and pulp and that will stop the diarrhea."

"Nandu, Kanchi wants to speak with you. Could you please come?" cried Rita.

I walked in and could not believe how much worse she looked in such a short time. Her small face was pale and sweaty, and her eyes had lost their sparkle.

I leaned over and whispered in her ear, "Kanchi, please try to rest. I will be right back." I knew that she was sinking fast. As I got up to leave, she motioned for me to come close. I put my ear next to her mouth.

I could barely hear her words. "Nandu, if I die, please do not cremate me. Bury me next to Devi Kali."

I thought the scraping of rocks on the axles of Father Autry's Land Rover were sure to break them on the road to Bichia. We decided to take a shortcut on the rougher road south to the border. We passed the spot where Dilly and I had found the oxcart holding Kanchi and the girls only four months ago: A lifetime seemed to have passed since then. But I did not have time to think about it. I looked across at Indra in the backseat with me. He was the bravest boy I knew, but even he was fighting back tears.

Father Autry spoke in Hindi to the Indian border guards, and explained why this was such an emergency. Even though we did not have the proper permits, they waved us through. A policeman hopped in back just in case to keep an eye on us.

"Dhan Bahadur, drive us straight to Dr. Aziz's house." The narrow lane made it almost impossible for the Land Rover to squeeze through.

A boy came to the door, a servant, and said Dr. Aziz had just left to go shopping. It was market day. We jumped back into the Land Rover and headed to the open-air market, which was thronged with people. It was not only market day, but it must also have been an Indian holiday. All the shops and stores lining the streets around the market were jammed with customers. How would we ever find him? My heart began to beat faster. We purchased ten ripe pomegranates.

"Indra, Father-*sahib*, I think we should fan out and look for him. We will meet back here in ten minutes," I said. What if the servant was wrong, or Dr. Aziz had changed his mind? I headed off to where we had first met him near the stall that sold the powdered milk. It was filled with shoppers.

Suddenly, the policeman who was walking with me grabbed my shoulder and pointed. He knew everyone in the small town.

"Dr. Aziz!" I shouted.

"Nandu!" He waved to me.

I ran to him. I did not waste a second telling him about Kanchi. "Nandu, drive me to my house so I can fetch my medical kit and some antibiotics."

We sped back to Dr. Aziz's house, navigating around people and cows lying in the street. Dr. Aziz returned in less than a minute, carrying his medical kit. He climbed back in the Land Rover. Just as we were about to leave, his kind, elderly father came out and offered us lemons to take back. I took them and held them in my lap—their strong yellow color gave me hope for Kanchi.

We dropped the border guard back at the checkpoint and thanked him. On the return, I had never driven so fast in a vehicle before. The leaves of forest trees became a green blur out the window. I kept thinking about Kanchi, about how much courage she showed from the moment we first found her tied together to the two sisters. I tried to tell myself, if anyone has the strength to hang on, it is her. It was hard to believe she was only ten years old.

We made it back to the stable before nightfall. When we pulled up in the twilight, none of us could believe our eyes. Surrounding *Subba-sahib*'s bungalow was a herd of elephants. When we approached, they parted for us to pass through the door. I could see that two of them had their trunks sticking through the open window, trying to sniff Kanchi. It was the little jumbo, Laxmi Kali, and the wild female squeezed in next to her that had had its leg freed from the snare.

Hira Prashad stood just outside the circle of elephants. He was agitated. The threat from the Maroons was over and he was King of the Borderlands again. But there was nothing in

253

his power to make Kanchi well. There were so few people he allowed to approach him, let alone sit on his back. Kanchi was one of the few.

I tried to reassure my elephant with *kuchis*. But he ignored them. "We will do everything to help her, Hira Prashad," I said. "Dr. Aziz is very skilled. We must hope that Kanchi comes back to us, like the tiger."

Rita pulled me aside. "Nandu, the elephants came up to the bungalow without a word. I hope your doctor can help. It feels like the elephants are already mourning her. I tried to push their trunks away from blocking the window, but Laxmi Kali would not leave nor would the wild female."

"They see Kanchi as part of their family," I said. I aspired to be a bridge between the wild and the human, but Kanchi had come to it naturally, without even trying.

———

Dr. Aziz sat by Kanchi's bedside for hours. Kabita and Jayanti were also immovable from her side. Dr. Aziz gave Kanchi three injections of antibiotics. I knew from Dilly that in Nepali mountain cultures like Jumla, people hold to the belief that a needle injection from a real doctor can cure anything.

"Now we just have to wait, Nandu," Jayanti said.

My father motioned me to his private grove, where we prayed together. Later the Baba joined us.

I said all of my prayers to Ban Devi. My father was deep in a trance and so was the Baba. I heard myself say quietly but out loud, "If Kanchi dies, I will never pray to anybody again."

I kept saying to myself, *I have already lost my mother, Devi Kali, I cannot lose Kanchi. Nor could Kabita and Jayanti, or Rita. They are sisters now.* And what would happen to poor Laxmi Kali? The little jumbo's heart would break to lose her best friend in the world. And the wild elephant herd had lost their bull. The jungle had lost Pradhan and twenty-four other rhinos.

The elephants from our stable and their wild friends also stayed by the bungalow, unwilling to eat or move. I slept in my hammock on the veranda of the barracks so I could be close by if help was needed. Dr. Aziz and Father Autry took turns watching over Kanchi. There was not a single person who was not part of the vigil. Even the drivers took turns checking in on her.

Sometimes in the Borderlands it goes from night to day in seconds. But sometimes, like this day, the dawn sky hangs so low that the morning takes ages to arrive. I walked over to the bungalow in this heavy morning light.

"There is no change, Nandu," Dr. Aziz said. He looked worried.

"Maybe that is a good thing?" I said, half question, half hope.

The truth was, ever since midnight, I had started to mourn

ERIC DINERSTEIN

her loss, by myself. I could not sleep and so I relived all my time with Kanchi, from the moment Hira Prashad rescued her from the back of the wagon to a few days ago, when she, Indra, Hira Prashad, and I set off to put a stop to the poachers. I remembered the song she had made up after we were captured and she was scared, the one she sang to cheer us both up. The one about the girl who is lost and crying in a mountain valley near Jumla and her elephant finds her and carries her home. I hoped that in the next life my Devi Kali would find Kanchi and take care of her like my elephant mother took care of me. I had never met anyone like Kanchi, someone I knew for such a short time but who had affected me so much. She was fearless, but this typhoid had struck her down.

The clouds broke into a morning rain shower that drenched the Borderlands. As the day wore on, the rain came down harder and harder, but still the elephants would not move from their circle around the bungalow.

My father motioned for me to come over to him. He was standing outside in the pouring rain. "Nandu, go in and pay your last respects. I do not think it will be long now."

I entered the bungalow and stood at the bottom of the cot looking up at her. I had forgotten how small she was lying on the large cot. Even over the past two days, in her illness she

256

seemed to be growing smaller as the typhoid took hold of her, trying to drag her into the earth.

I left to keep from breaking down in front of the girls and Indra, who sat on the edge of the cot. When I passed my father, I whispered, "We will bury her next to Devi Kali."

The afternoon wore on. I decided to make myself useful and so I began shucking the outer husk of the pomegranates. When I had filled a bowl with the seeds and red flesh, I brought them over to the bungalow. I expected to see the others file out at any moment.

I was making my way through the circle of elephants when I felt something familiar—a sense of the air vibrating. I could feel it around me. The elephants had started to rumble, and not just any rumble, but the happiest one they make, like when they slip into the river for their daily bath.

They knew it before we did. I rushed into the bungalow.

Kanchi opened her eyes. Her fever had broken.

THIRTY

With the care of her adopted sisters, and all of us, including Laxmi Kali (who rarely left Kanchi's side), Kanchi recovered quickly. She had joined me to place lemongrass on Devi Kali's grave, when I noticed the fruits in the giant fig tree by the banks of the Belgadi north of our stable had begun to ripen. The langur monkeys alerted us to them. We picked some fresh figs off the ground and walked back to the stable, where we fed them to Hira Prashad. My great tusker now lived at the stable only part-time. He was part of the wild herd, too, and would be gone for days at a time.

When he had finished the figs, Hira Prashad began to walk down to the Belgadi River south of our stable. I followed to see him join his other herd. He rumbled to them where they were splashing in the river, and they left the water to join him. I kept my distance, but watched them turn around to head right through the center of camp. They had not been back since Kanchi's illness.

My father, too, did nothing but sit and watch from his spot in the gazebo. Our elephants standing inside their enclosure started to rumble loudly. Prem Kali led them to the metal gate. After the capture of the poachers, I talked to my father and convinced him that we no longer needed to shackle the elephants' legs with chains and treat them like prisoners. A wire fence with three strands proved enough to keep them in the corral at night. *Subba-sahib* gave the order for the drivers to open the gate. The stable elephants joined their wild cousins and headed off. It was not until they were nearly at Devi Kali's gravesite that I realized Hira Prashad was leading them under the fig tree.

Rita and I slipped through the rumbling herds and raced to climb it. We started to shake branches and cut the clumps of fruit to feed the happy elephants squeaking with delight below us. Soon Kanchi, Indra, and my father were there to watch, too. Kanchi shouted, "Come down, Nandu, we have to feed the little jumbos. Their trunks are too clumsy to pick up these figs."

Looking down on the elephants rumbling and reaching for their fruits, I felt something grab me inside. I used to think that my favorite view of the world was overlooking the Great Sand Bar River and gazing from my elephant's back to the waves of grass blowing in the breeze. Now I realized that the best view was right here, looking down on all the elephants, my friends, my family.

I will never know the God who made this world—Animist, the Buddhist, the Hindu, the Muslim, or my tutor's God—so I thanked them all.

We humans like to think that we are above animals, smarter and more clever, but we are animals, too. When I look at my fellow human animals, I don't understand what makes some of us do what we do: the poachers, the villagers who would have speared the Baba's tiger, the fathers of Kabita and Jayanti and of Kanchi. But when I remember that we are all animals, trying to make our way in the world, I understand a little bit. And that little bit of understanding can give way to a greater understanding. I believe this is how horrible things can be stopped, reversed, forgiven. Tomorrow, we can always start again, take a new path.

I thought of the lonely elephant calling to the humpback whales. I pictured him so clearly now, standing on the mountain ridge, calling out to his animal family, trumpeting loudly, mourning his loss, warning of risk, asking for understanding.

At last, I answered his call. "We heard you. You can rest now. We will defend you. We will defend you all."

IMPORTANT TERMS

bhanti—a kind of mint plant from which a healing powder is made

Bichia—the border town on the Indian side from the Borderlands and the largest bazaar

Borderlands, the—the low flat land (elevation around six hundred feet) along the border between Nepal and India at the base of the Himalayas; where this story takes place. There are three officials of different ranks who are assigned to the Borderlands:

> **forest conservator-*sahib***—Mr. Rijal, who oversees all of the forests of western Nepal
>
> **warden-*sahib***—Mr. Dhungel, who is the chief warden or wildlife officer for the Borderlands reserve and reports to Mr. Rijal
>
> **game scout**—"Ganesh Lal," an assistant to Mr. Dhungel

Budghar—the headman in a Tharu village

caste system—In Nepal, people are divided into castes or ranks, with the Hindu Brahmins as highest caste and Tharus and Tamangs of low caste or status; elephant drivers are almost always of low caste; level of education also often follows caste

chapatti—flat bread, often eaten in place of rice

daju—literally *older brother*, but a term that can be used affectionately for any boy who is familiar and older than you

dhole—another common name for the Asiatic wild dog; a wild canid that hunts in packs and is common in the Borderlands

didi—literally *older sister*, but a term that can be used affectionately for any girl who is familiar and older than you

Diwali—also called Tihar in Nepal, the festival of light, the most important festival of the year for Hindus

driver—each elephant in the stable has three drivers:

    phanit—the head driver

    pachuwa—the second-in-command of the elephant

    mahout—the entry-level driver

gharial—an ancient endangered member of the crocodile family, now found only in the Borderlands and a few other places

Gurkhas—the name of the Nepali army regiment recruited by the British

Kali—the last name of every female elephant; Kali refers to a female life-form and also a flower blossom

kuchi—the Nepali word for elephant treats consisting of unhusked rice, rock salt, and crude sugar wrapped in leaves or elephant grass

kukhri—the traditional curved knife used by Nepali men and made famous by the British Gurkha soldiers

lungis—a long piece of cotton wrapped around the waist and legs, like a sarong

namaste—the traditional greeting among Nepalis, meaning literally "I bow to the God in you"

Prashad (also **Prasad**)—the last name of male elephants

pudinah—another kind of mint plant from which a healing powder is made

puja—a ceremony of worship

raksi—the home-distilled rice wine of the Borderlands

Raute—the name of the last wandering tribe of hunter-gatherers in Nepal (pronounced Rauté)

rupee—the name of the currency in Nepal

sadhu—the Nepali name for a Hindu holy man

sahib—similar to "sir," the word that Nepali and Indians attach to titles or names to show respect (for example, one might refer to a teacher as teacher-*sahib*)

sal—the most common tree of lowland Nepal and North India

samosa—a triangular, deep-fried turnover filled with vegetables and spices

sel roti—the special bread eaten during Diwali

shaman—a person with special powers who can engage spirits, use magic, and foretell the future

Subba-sahib (pronounced **Sooba-saheb**)—title given to the officer in charge of an elephant stable

Tharu—the indigenous people of the Borderlands

Tihar—the five-day Hindu festival of light, typically falling after the rice harvest

tika—in the Hindu religion a mark of colored dye placed as a blessing in the middle of the forehead

topi—the traditional hat worn by most Nepali men and all government officials

tusker—a bull elephant that sports huge ivory

Common Elephant Commands Used by the Drivers

agat—forward

beit—kneel down

chhi—let alone; drop

hikh—attack; close in sideways

kun—dig with your trunk

meil—get up

pasar—kneel over to one side

raa—stand squarely and stop what you are doing

AUTHOR'S NOTE

When I was a young boy growing up in New Jersey, tigers, rhinos, and elephants were my favorite animals, but they lived only in my imagination. I encountered them firsthand when I joined the Peace Corps in 1975 and landed in Nepal. My job was to census tigers and other wildlife, on foot—no elephants to ride or a Hira Prashad to protect me. Over the ensuing decades my career as a wildlife biologist took me all over the world and far from my roots in the Borderlands jungles. Writing novels about a young Nepali elephant driver would have to wait.

A Circle of Elephants focuses on two powerful, opposing themes, one I wish to promote and the other I am devoted to stopping. The first is the awe young people hold for wild animals and a deep desire to protect them from harm. The second is the incredible cruelty shown by a small minority of people who kill rhinos, tigers, elephants, and many other species of wildlife for profit. This novel is staged in the past, at a time when the poaching of rhinos and tigers still occurred in Nepal. Today, however, Nepal is a world leader in wildlife protection—barely any tigers, rhinos, or elephants have been poached during recent years. Government officers, park rangers, and the people of Nepal deserve tremendous credit for stopping this scourge.

I had to look elsewhere for inspiration, where the struggle to protect wildlife is most dire. I wrote much of the second draft of this novel while working on the western edge of Africa's most iconic wildlife park, the Serengeti. Here, the world's greatest animal migration takes place every year when millions of wildebeest, zebra, and Cape buffalo follow the rains over the grassy plains from northern Tanzania to southern Kenya and back again. I was there to introduce a new kind of technology to help prevent the poaching that threatens one of the natural wonders of the world. Before dawn I would wake to write and sometimes, in the quiet, I could hear the yapping of hyenas and the moan of lions, the voices of wildness. It is the same thrill that runs through me when I hear the wild elephants trumpet in the jungles of my beloved Borderlands.

The commitment of a few dedicated individuals—like those portrayed in this novel and in real life—can make all the difference against what seems like overwhelming odds. We have to speak up like Nandu, Kanchi, and *Subba-sahib* to save these magnificent animals who have no voice in their own futures.

Eric Dinerstein

ACKNOWLEDGMENTS

This novel is set in the jungles that were once called the Royal Karnali-Bardia Wildlife Reserve (now Bardia National Park). I would like to acknowledge the Peace Corps for placing me there and the staff, especially the late Gagan Singh, for their support. Five years of research on tigers and rhinos and riding elephants in Chitwan informed this book. I want to thank the Smithsonian Tiger Ecology Project for sponsoring my work and the education and company offered by our outstanding trackers and elephant drivers—Vishnu Lama, Harka Man Lama, Bul Bahadur Lama, Man Bahadur Lama, Ram Kumar Aryal, Man Singh, and Keshav Giri, Gyan Bahadur Tharu, Bir Bahadur Lama, Phirta Tharu, Brij Lal Tharu, Pashupat Tharu, Badri Tharu, Ram Raj Tharu, Arjun Kumal, Maila Kumal, Ram Bahadur Gurung, and Ram Ji Tharu. Hemanta Mishra—my former boss, colleague, and a founding father of Nepali wildlife conservation—shared his insights about the people and the wildlife of his country and made excellent comments on a late draft. Katya and Amelia Gonzalez influenced the creation of Kanchi as a character in the novel.

Without the wonderful support of Steve D'Esposito and my colleagues at Resolve, Inc., especially Nathan Hahn, Steve Gulick, and Sanjiv Fernando, I would not be able to advance my mission to protect endangered wildlife or find time to write this novel. Nancy Sherman, Paige Grant, John Lehmkuhl, Pat Emmert, Holly Dinerstein, Trishna Gurung, Anup Joshi, and Shubash Lohani were close readers and editors. Annie Bruno edited several drafts of this book and was an invaluable source of ideas and insights into local color and the characters. She helped shape this novel and I am indebted. My agent, Richard Abate, has been an enthusiastic supporter of my efforts to introduce Nandu's world to a wide audience. Best of all, he found me the perfect editor for middle-grade fiction, Tracey Keevan at Disney Hyperion, who shares my love of animals and passion for wildlife conservation. I am in awe of her extraordinary editing talent and so thankful for the time she devoted to bringing this story to life. Finally, I would like to thank another close reader, my wife, Ute, whose sharp eyes and patience made all the difference.